SHOOTING BOGIES

SHOOTING BOGIES

A Novel

Ralph Monti

Copyright © 2024 Ralph Monti

All rights reserved.
No part of this book may be reproduced or transmitted in any form or by any electronic or mechanical means, including photocopying, recording, or by any information storage and retrieval system without the written permission of the publisher.

This is a work of fiction. Names, characters, places, and incidents either are the product of the author's imagination or are used fictitiously and any resemblance to actual persons, living or dead, businesses, companies, events or locales is entirely coincidental.

Print edition ISBN 979-8-218-36892-0
E-Book ISBN 979-8-218-37837-0

Cover design by Mark Montgomery

Acknowledgments

There are several people who took the time to provide feedback, suggest ideas, and find pesky typos that infiltrated (by my hand!) the manuscript. I can't thank them enough for their friendship and support. They include Lee Baldwin, Alan Felsen, Tom Roberts, Jeanne Staab, Bill Telgheder, and Barbara and Steve Zammarchi.

And to my wife, Margaret, who I have been blessed to have by my side. She is, and always will be, my first reader.

Also by Ralph Monti

Remember Brooklyn: Memories From Famous Sons and Daughters

Bet on Your Golf Game! An Indispensable Guide for Betting On the Golf Course

*Career Opportunities in Magazine Publishing: The Ultimate Guide to Succeeding in The Business

The Creative Salesperson: How to Develop Your Creativity Into an Effective Sales Tool

*Publishers Marketing Association Benjamin Franklin award winner for Career Writing

For my son, John-Carlo.
What joy and inspiration you brought
to my life!
You are forever here.

1

Thursday, May 1

Rocky Delmonico slammed down the phone and screamed, "Holy shit, I'm dead!" He pulled at hair matted against his oversized head. The phone rang again, and Rocky almost jumped through his skin.

"Rocky, whattaya a fuckin' moron or what?" a gravelly voice on the line said.

Rocky's brain was frying. His face was bright red. Sweat was spilling down his nose. The new sleeveless tee he bought last week at Kohl's, part of a three-pack special, was soaked, clinging to his bulky mass like a sopping wet carwash towel. How had he gotten himself into this friggin' mess?

The gravelly voice belonged to Louie Perello, known as The Pipe, because he was so skinny. He was Rocky's best friend since childhood, but Rocky knew The Pipe was calling him on orders from Gino Lofaccio.

"Louie, I screwed up. Ya gotta help me. I just got off the phone with Crazy Vinnie."

"I don't know what I can do right now, Rocky. Gino's pissed big-time, you laughing at his mother like that."

"It came out wrong," Rocky said. "I just started laughing, Pipe, but not directly at the old biddy."

"Rocky, ya gotta go see Gino right away. He's askin' for you, and no from you is not an answer he wants to hear right now. He told me to get your fat ass here pronto."

"I can't come right now, Pipe. I gotta take my mother to the doc's," Rocky said. "She's got the gout again."

"Rocco!" screamed Louie's raspy voice. "Screw your mother and her gout. She's gotta wait. Don't mess with Gino, Rocco. You know how he is."

Rocky wanted to tell The Pipe to shove it, first for calling him Rocco, which The Pipe did when he acted like his higher-than-mighty big brother. And then for telling him to temporarily ice his mother because he had to kiss Gino's ass and make things right. But Rocky knew The Pipe was right. Gino was a nutcase. He knew what he had done was serious, him laughing at Gino's mother, especially during the funeral. The Pipe was only trying to protect him from Gino's wacko temper.

"Alright, Pipe," Rocky said. "Tell Gino I'll be there in an hour. I gotta get cleaned up first."

"I'll see you at Gino's," Louie said.

Rocky stared into the faded mirror hanging above the old-fashioned mahogany table that held the phone. His mother had already lit her four votive candles. They flickered quietly in their frosted glass holders. The table was his mother's family shrine. It was 2 p.m., and he was already exhausted. Rocky hadn't gotten to church but would have to ice Mass, too. Something he did a few mornings a week. Too bad, Rocky thought. He hoped to see the cute blond whose husband was laid up in the hospital. She had great booty and a sizeable rack, and he enjoyed giving her the sign of peace when he got the chance. But that wasn't happening today. He had bigger things to worry about than hounding some hot tail who sat in the third pew at St. Catherine's.

He couldn't believe how the day was turning out. Not three hours ago, he was all dressed up in his best suit, a $1,500 Zegna he paid only $300 for, to Johnny Back Door. It was one of Johnny's better scores. It was part of a huge truckload of duds heading to Neiman Marcus at the Garden State Plaza Mall. Over a couple of shots at the Black Rock

Shooting Bogies

Bar on Bloomfield Avenue, Johnny told him how he liked jumping into rigs parked at the Vince Lombardi Rest Area on the New Jersey Turnpike and driving off. Johnny never knew what he scored until he opened the box. Kinda sloppy, but kinda exciting too, Johnny said. Stealing rigs like that was like opening Christmas presents; you never know what you stole until you opened the back doors. Meat. Clothing. Furniture. One time it was a container of caskets that Johnny sold to a funeral director in Passaic County.

Rocky drew a deep breath and looked at the old, faded photo of his father that sat quietly on his mother's homemade shrine table.

"Pop," Rocky whispered to the withered, sepia-tinged photo, "I screwed up today with the wrong people. Say a little prayer for me up there. I'm going to need your help."

He scanned the rest of the table. It was decorated with dead relative photos: His father, Rocco Sr., Uncle Sal, Aunt Philomena, his cousin Joey, Anthony Corrone, his grandfather, grandma Susie, his sister Renata, and Lucky, the family's first dog. How mamma cried when Lucky died, Rocky thought. During a July thunderstorm, the poor mutt got fried when his front paw touched a downed electrical line under a rhododendron in the backyard. Even the family dog took it on the chin, Rocky thought.

Standing squarely in the middle of the photo gallery were three-foot statues of a blue-gowned Madonna and a heart-glowing Jesus. Rocky won both statues at the St. Catherine's Annual Bazaar when he was eight. Despite being chubby, Rocky was one of the neighborhood's better athletes. He won Mary and Jesus by shooting ten free-throw baskets in a row. Although his mother gushed and beamed at her little Rocco that night, those statues have come to haunt him ever since. Their eternal stillness, especially at night with all the lights out, always spooked

Shooting Bogies

Rocky. They triggered creepy, superstitious, bogeyman feelings. Then his mother got it into her head to build a shrine around the statues. First, adding the votive candles and then photos of dead relatives as they all began to die.

He remembered peeking at her makeshift shrine from the nearby sofa bed where he slept. The eerie glowing-heart statue of Jesus, accented by the flickering votive candles and the dead relative photos, gave the room a bizarre vibe. He began keeping a stockpile of rubber bands under his pillow. He'd shoot them at the evil spirits lurking in the dark when he'd get spooked. His mother always yelled at him to pick up all the rubber bands strewn on her white shag rug. He never told her what they were for. And she never asked.

The dead of night was so scary that he kept a nightlight on when he slept. As much as the room spooked him, though, there was no way he'd ever move into his sister's room after she died. Even if he wanted to, which he didn't since that would mean him sleeping in a dead person's bed, his mother would never have allowed it.

Rocky looked at Renata's photo. She would be 43 now, Rocky figured, nine years older than him. What a beautiful young girl she had become, Rocky thought. Slim like his mother. Long dark hair, glistening white teeth. She inherited all the good looks from both his mother and father. Good looks ran in the family. But somehow, they missed him. Something he figured out a long time ago. As far back as he could remember, he was always short and chubby. The neighborhood kids made fun of him. The nuns had little patience for him. Even his favorite teacher, Mrs. Dreyfus, a high school homeroom teacher whom he had a crush on, often called him Pudge. No PC sensitivity back in the day in Belleville, New Jersey. Those times hurt.

Shooting Bogies

His saving grace was that he was the neighborhood ace in sports. At least he had something he could be proud of there.

The telephone rang again.

"Yeah," Rocky said, disguising his voice.

"Rocky?" the voice asked.

"Yeah?"

"Rocky, it's me, Howard."

"Hey, Howard," Rocky said, relieved it wasn't one of Gino's boys calling again. "How ya doin'?"

"Doing great, man," Howard said. "How about you? You answered the phone funny. Thought I dialed the wrong number."

"Nah, you just caught me thinking," Rocky replied. "What's up?" Rocky asked, trying to move the conversation along as he checked his watch.

"You know those two Asian guys I introduced you to last week on the practice green at the Misty River tournament?" Howard asked. "They're looking for a golf game with some serious action. They're talking about $3,000 Nassaus and probably some side games to spice things up."

"So when do we play."

"We got an 8:30 tee time this Saturday at the club," Howard said. "Should be money in the bank. You good for 8:30?"

"Yeah, I'm good, Rocky said. "See you then."

Rocky looked at his watch again. He had less than an hour to get to Gino's.

2

While Rocky was dressing, he thought about the number one rule in Belleville, New Jersey: Never screw around with Gino Lofaccio or his crazy mother, Anna.

Since the time Gino was a little kid raging a campaign of terror against his schoolmates in St. Catherine's Elementary School, all that anyone remembers about Gino was how much of a prick he was. He was a tough little bastard who would punch you out in a New York City heartbeat. Kids of all sizes and shapes were afraid of Gino, who, despite his short stature, ruled any class and schoolyard he stepped into. As time passed, Gino grew to just under five feet, four inches tall like his mother. But height was not the only thing Gino inherited from her. Gino's scumbag gene came from Anna, a nasty, hot-tempered nutcase of a woman who would take on anyone who dared or was stupid enough to cross her path.

Mrs. Lofaccio's run-ins and fights were part of Belleville lore. There was a time when she angrily slashed the tires of a car whose owner dared to park in front of the Lofaccio home. It didn't matter that the vehicle belonged to an unsuspecting doctor who had recently moved into the neighborhood from Davenport, Iowa, and had no idea of the brutality of the Lofaccio clan of Belleville, New Jersey.

When he first moved to Montague Street, the sallow, bespectacled doctor quickly made friends in the neighborhood. He was known for his generosity of time, talent, and spirit. Between his shifts at the nearby Clara Maass Hospital, he often made emergency house calls to neighbors, especially tending to the cancer-riddled Mr. DiBovi up the street. He was a regular churchgoer at St. Catherine's and always attended the 10:00 a.m. Sunday Mass. He volunteered with the grammar school baseball team, although he wasn't married and had no kids. Most people in Belleville called him The Hawkeye Saint. But despite his reputation and human goodness, Gino and his friends would call him a queer when he walked by. They'd pull nasty pranks and mock and jeer his midwestern accent. The doctor would smile and move on. Through his Montague Street neighbors, the doctor soon learned about the crazy Lofaccio family. But people never got around to telling the good doctor the neighborhood's second rule, which was as sacred as the first: Never, *ever* park in front of the Lofaccio house. Of course, nobody had the guts to question Mrs. Lofaccio why she didn't want you parking in front of her home. It was one of her unwritten neighborhood laws that just existed, and that was that.

Rocky recalled the long-ago summer afternoon when Mrs. Lofaccio dragged Sean McGrath by his hair halfway down the street. Poor Sean was a newly arrived, freckled-faced immigrant kid from Ireland. A kid who Rocky immediately liked and befriended.

It was a hot July afternoon. All the kids were out in the street playing stickball. Joey Eyeglasses was pitching. In came a pitch, and Sean, who's at bat, scorched the pink Spaldeen foul straight into the head of an imported ceramic Madonna statue on the Lofaccio front lawn. In the time it took to say "Hail Mary, full of grace," the statue's head flew off in a snap.

While all the kids screamed and fell to the ground with glee, laughing and marveling at the one-in-a-million odds of Sean's line drive (Rocky remembering that he laughed so hard he peed in his pants) out shot Mrs. Lofaccio from behind her screened front door.

Shooting Bogies

Meanwhile, poor Sean, who didn't know a foul ball from a screwball, furiously rounded the bases, incomprehensively thinking he had a chance at a home run, making the kids laugh even harder. And just as poor Sean triumphantly stomped on the sewer cover that was designated as home plate, Mrs. Lofaccio, her eyes bulging, forehead veins popping, and her mouth spewing four-letter curses, greeted poor Sean at home plate with a sudden and violent kick that landed squarely into Sean's 13-year-old "gentles." As Sean crumpled over in sheer agony, Mrs. Lofaccio grabbed a handful of his hair, dragged him down the street to deposit the writhing boy onto his front stoop, and furiously punched the front door of the McGrath home. It took the McGrath family almost four months to pay for a replacement. Mrs. Lofaccio had a new imported Madonna gracing her front lawn by Christmas.

The real masterpiece of Mrs. LoFaccio's insanity, however, was an incident that brought Rocky himself face-to-face with the neighborhood's most feared and crazed woman.

Montague was usually a quiet street, just as the Lofaccio clan liked and demanded it to be. That all changed one summer when a wild and wooly kid named Anthony Lorenzo moved in down the block with his mother and his maxed-out Mustang. Anthony spent hours in Mrs. McGarrity's garage at the end of Montague working on his midnight-blue ride. He would pour all the hard-earned money he made at the local ShopRite into the latest aftermarket parts to make his Stang gallop faster. And it seemed that after every part Anthony installed, he would have the urge to time-trial his metal beast down Montague at speeds topping over 100 mph.

Shooting Bogies

To alert the neighborhood kids playing stickball on the street that he was ready for one of his test runs, Anthony would rev the Stang's turbocharged powerplant to deafening RPMs, rattling the windows of half the houses on the block. That signaled the kids to clear the street and find a seat atop the stoops and fences. It was like the Red Sea parting for Moses. The kids loved Anthony's time trials and found them an exciting summer evening highlight. The neighborhood adults thought otherwise, especially Mrs. Lofaccio, who was already on the outs with the Lorenzo family. She viewed Anthony's test runs as dangerous and disturbing to the peaceful tranquility of the neighborhood. But more importantly, they defied her absolute control of the street.

So on a hot, humid, dusky August evening, Anthony Lorenzo and his souped-up Stang throttled down the street like a proverbial bat out of hell. And walking down the sidewalk coming the other way was

Mrs. Lofaccio, a box of DelVecchio Bakery pastries in her hand. And between these two opposing forces sat 14-year-old Rocco Delmonico, happily perched on his family's stoop. As Anthony's screaming ride rocketed closer and closer, Rocco couldn't help but notice Mrs. Lofaccio furiously tearing off the little red string tied around the bleached-white pastry box.

With a force as sudden and angry as the Stang's maxed-out engine wailing on all its turbocharged cylinders, Mrs. Lofaccio stepped up to the curb. She hurled the now-open bakery box containing two napoleons, four éclairs, and six cannoli at Anthony Lorenzo and his speeding Mustang. As often happens on Montague Street, Mrs. Lofaccio scored a direct hit, the barrage of her pastry artillery flying through the open driver's side window and hitting Anthony square in the face. Not two seconds after Mrs. Lofaccio's perfect score, a riot of glistening red sparks

Shooting Bogies

followed by ugly sounds of crushing metal filled the air as the out-of-control Mustang bounced back and forth against the opposite rows of parked cars that lined the curbs of Montague Street.

Luckily, Anthony escaped unharmed, but his poor Mustang was totaled. Of course, no one in the neighborhood saw or knew anything when the cops arrived, especially little Rocco Delmonico. Because after flinging her pastries, Anna Lofaccio coldly watched the spectacular crash. Once satisfied and sated by the result, she turned around and looked Rocco square in the eye with a witch-like sneer. Her look said it all, and Rocky's flesh crawled. He knew even *think*ing about ratting her out to the police would be a huge mistake.

Rocky swore right then and there to never, *ever* screw around with the Lofaccios. And for over 20 years, he avoided pissing them off until this very day. With one uncontrollable move, Rocky had inadvertently walked into the crosshairs of both Gino and Mrs. Lofaccio. And now he had to pay for it.

3

"Rocco," a somber-faced Pipe said as he opened the door to the Lofaccio home. The Pipe acted like somebody died, which somebody did, and Rocky was hoping he wouldn't be next.

"Pipe," Rocky answered just as somberly. "How's it goin'?"

"I'm doin' okay, Rocco. Come in. Gino's downstairs. Sit in the living room, Rocco," The Pipe said, motioning to a worn, high-back, upholstered chair inside the musty room. "I'll check with Gino and see if he's ready to see you."

Rocky didn't like the way The Pipe had greeted him. All serious. Calling him Rocco instead of Rocky. No chitchat. When The

Pipe was playing that role, it usually meant Gino, Mrs. Lofaccio, or both were on the warpath.

Rocky sat and waited. His heart was thumping. He could feel it knocking against the St. Francis of Assisi medal he wore around his neck. His oversized palms felt like wet sponges. Considering the circumstances, he'd be sweating in the freakin' shower.

He had to make things right with Gino and Mrs. Lofaccio. He did what he always swore he wouldn't do: He'd crossed the line with these lunatics. Now, he had to apologize, show respect, ask what he could do to make things right, and hope he left in one piece.

Was it twenty years since he was last in this house? Not what you would expect being inside the home of one of New Jersey's mob families. While a ruthless asshole, Gino was smart enough to know better than flaunt his dough.

Shooting Bogies

For Gino, it wasn't the money that got him juiced. It was power. Little Gino loved control more than money. His ego was stoked when he was scaring people.

Rocky sat and noticed how uninviting the house was—no pictures or photos hanging on the walls. The room was almost bare except for the shabby furniture. The chair he was sitting on was lumpy. And there was a worn ivy-colored couch bookended by chipped mahogany tables dating back to the Mussolini years. Two old lamps stood on each table. Neither was lighted.

Sun-faded curtains hung against the windows and were shut tight. Their scrunched tops looked like they were strangling each other. The Lofaccios had never opened those curtains as far back as Rocky could remember. From the outside, the Lofaccio house gave off a hostile, closed aura, eerily personifying the two hard-edged personalities within. The only thing warm about the Lofaccio house was the impeccably sculpted Madonna that stood serenely on the Lofaccio lawn. That and the bordering rose bush, which bore rich summer blooms that radiated a bright-red brilliance. But Sean McGrath made the Madonna a Belleville legend, and neglect eventually killed off the rose bush.

"Rocco," the Pipe called from the darkened hallway, "Gino's ready to see you."

Rocky jumped up, straightened his suit and tie, and followed The Pipe down the stairs where Gino was waiting.

Although there were three levels to the Lofaccio home, the underground basement level of 18 Montague Street was the operations and daily living center of the Lofaccio clan.

Only Gino's closest men, according to The Pipe, were allowed down the stairs to the three rooms where Gino and Mrs. Lofaccio coordinated their business. The second floor, where Rocky sat waiting, was used for short, informal meetings. Like talking to a shopkeeper who was late on a protection payment. Or discussing a minor indiscretion an associate might have committed. The third floor, where Gino and Mrs. Lofaccio lived, was off-limits to everybody. No one was allowed up to the third floor, not even the closest of friends or relatives. Rocky instinctively knew that by going downstairs, he was in deep shit. He was looking at some serious face time with Gino.

Gino sat in the darkened room behind a desk. To his right stood Crazy Vinnie Bellomo, Gino's primary enforcer. Vinnie was a barbell-pumping freak whose muscles bulged through his black suit, the suit he wore to this morning's funeral. Rocky knew Vinnie forever. From his early teenage years, Vinnie was the toughest kid in Belleville, tougher than Gino but without his future boss's smarts. Vinnie spent his teenage years itching for fights. In elementary school, he sang Italian arias at the neighborhood feasts. He had a soaring operatic voice, and everyone agreed that Vincenzo Bellomo was destined for the stage. But when Vinnie turned 13, his life changed. First, Vinnie's old man got thrown into the slammer for a twenty-year murder charge. Then Mrs. Bellomo, a barmaid at the Blue Dot Bar and Grill, died of a pulmonary embolism. So Vinnie was left to fend for himself with an old spinster aunt who came to live in his house. Soon Vinnie was pissed off all the time, venting his anger through his fists.

Instead of being known as an opera prodigy who belted out arias from Lucia De Lammamoor, he morphed into an angry street thug who belted people around for kicks. And before long, he was hanging out with little Gino Lofaccio. Being Gino's enforcer was a job right up Vinnie's alley. It was a perfect fit for his rage. No reason to read *What Color Is Your Parachute?* for Vinnie.

Shooting Bogies

"Sit there," Vinnie said to Rocky, pointing a meaty hand to a chair directly in front of Gino, who was busy signing some papers. After a short time, Gino looked up. A long, eerie silence seemed to linger forever as Gino stared into Rocky's eyes.

"You embarrassed and laughed at my family today, Rocky," Gino said.

"I know, Gino. And I want to apologize to you and your mother for how I acted," Rocky said, going right into the apology act, not wasting any time. "I have the highest respect for you and your mother. I insulted both of you, and I am very sorry. I'll do whatever I can to make it right, Gino. I think you know me well enough, Gino. We go back a long time."

Yet another long silence made Rocky's response hang in the air. Rocky was wilting under Gino's icy, blue-eyed stare, a look very much like a cobra ready to strike. If he's looking for fear, Rocky thought, I sure as shit can't be disappointing. Rocky felt his fear gushing through his eyes and throat. His ears were ringing. His stomach was churning, and he was doing all he could not to lose control of his bladder. Believe me, Gino, Rocky told himself I'm scared shitless here.

Finally, Gino leaned forward and whispered: "Did you know that what my mother did at my father's funeral today is a tradition in the Lofaccio family? Something that goes back to their old village? Something that we Lofaccios hold sacred. Something that shouldn't be laughed at—ever!" The "ever" emphasized with a violent pounding of Gino's fist on his desk, causing a bobble-headed Frank Sinatra doll Gino kept nearby to jump up three to four inches.

"I found that out after. The Pipe here told me as I was walking back to my car," Rocky whispered back, ignoring the still bobbing, smiling head of The Chairman of the Board.

Shooting Bogies

"And you didn't think of coming over to apologize right away?" Gino asked. "I didn't think you were such a fuckin' idiot, Rocky."

"I didn't think it was the right time, Gino," Rocky said. "I was going to call as soon as I got home. But after I came through the door, the phone was already ringing. Vinnie told me to keep my afternoon open and that you wanted to see me. Then The Pipe called right after that to tell me the time."

Rocky couldn't believe he was in this deep over his laughing at some wacky old-world tradition. He didn't want to replay the image of Mrs. Lofaccio, a 65-year-old woman, but still spry as an aggressive pit bull puppy, jumping into her dead husband's grave. He may break out laughing again.

All he could think of was how this beautiful day in May had soured. Instead of going to an early morning Mass to catch a glimpse of that hot blond in the third pew and then being on the golf course with Howard hustling a couple of hackers out of some serious coin, he was standing near a dirt pile in a cemetery in Newark, attending the funeral of Biaggio Lofaccio, the patriarch of the Lofaccio clan. Some decrepit old geezer who had kicked the bucket three nights ago ruined a perfectly planned day.

Since Rocky could remember, Mr. Lofaccio was in and out of hospitals. He was more in hospitals than out. And for the last ten years, the old guy was institutionalized in a facility in Morris County. But when The Pipe called earlier in the week to tell Rocky the old man had finally kicked, he knew he had to pay his respects. The Lofaccios kept score. They would know who from the neighborhood attended and who didn't. And Rocky wanted to make sure he stayed on the right side of the Lofaccio ledger.

So there was Rocky, watching Crazy Vinnie Bellomo and his bulky cohorts lowering Biaggio Lofaccio's last remains into the moist earth of St. John's cemetery under the pious gaze of Monsignor John Russo. Rocky was relieved that the funeral was ending and fighting not to look at his watch.

But then, suddenly, here came a wailing and screaming Mrs. Lofaccio, flying through the air! And with a crisp metallic thud, the old biddy landed squarely onto the gleaming, gold casket six feet below. Poor Rocky began laughing uncontrollably. And who could blame him? Watching Mrs. Lofaccio fly through the air, Michael Jordan-style, and nail a perfect landing on a custom-made $25,000 casket will break the funeral tension for any highly superstitious person like Rocky Delmonico.

Rocky's out-of-control laughter immediately moved everyone into a cold and horrified communal silence, creating a graveside quiet as soundless as Biaggio Lofaccio's withered, old bones down below. Rocky's gaze met with none other than Gino Lofaccio's steely blue eyes as he worked to quiet his unrestrained guffawing. And if outrage could kill, Rocky Delmonico would have been whacked on the spot. Seemingly mocking Gino's mother while she performed a time-honored ritual made him a Lofaccio enemy.

So here he was now, facing some terrible Gino music.

"Rocky," Gino whispered, breaking Rocky's reverie. " There's no excuse for what you did today. You will have to pay."

"I'll do anything it takes to make it right, Gino," Rocky said.

"That's good, Rocky, that's very good. I'm glad to hear you say that," Gino said. "Anything less, and that would have been bad news. You've been saying all the right things."

"I didn't mean any disrespect, Gino," Rocky said.

"This is how you will make it right," Gino said. " I've got something I want you to do. It's been something I've been wanting to ask you to do for over a week. Now, I am no longer asking. It's an important job, but I don't want to discuss it now. I want you to meet me Monday night at my club in Newark. Be there at 9:00 p.m. Vinnie will show you in through the back door."

"Okay, Gino. Whatever you say. Thank you for letting me make this up to you," Rocky said. "Is your mother around? I want to apologize to her."

"She's been standing right behind you all this time," Gino said. "You can apologize now."

Rocky got up from the chair and turned to look at Mrs. Lofaccio. Although she stood just over five feet tall, he felt her inner fury lashing through him. He experienced the same intensity when he watched her throw that box of DelVecchio Bakery pastries at Anthony Lorenzo's head more than twenty years ago.

"Mrs. Lofaccio," Rocky began, "I'm genuinely sorry for my actions. I apologize for what I did today. I hope you can find it in your heart to forgive me."

Giving no clue how she'd respond, Anna Lofaccio stared quietly at Rocky through her bronze-smoked eyeglasses. Her mouth was tightly pursed. Rocky couldn't see her eyes but felt them burning holes through his skull. The room was dead silent. Then suddenly, and without warning, Rocky began to feel hot stings whipping across his right cheek and then another across his left cheek. At first, he was confused about what was causing him pain. Then he realized the old biddy was slapping the shit out of him. At first, he felt the natural inclination to step away. But then he decided to stand there and take it and resist the urge to fend off her blows. The slapping lasted an eternity. His face was red-hot and stinging, but he made no move to stop her. He knew this was part of his punishment.

After an interminable amount of time, she finally stopped slapping his face. She stared

Shooting Bogies

and looked up at him, and Rocky got ready for a swift kick to his nuts. He squeezed his bowels and tried to draw in his dick. To his surprise, she reached up to him instead and grabbed him hard by both his ears, squaring his reddened face to hers, and drew him close.

He stood there wondering what this little witch would do next. Without saying a word or warning, out of her mouth came a phlegmy glob that landed across his crimson-red face, smearing his eyes. She pushed back his face, released her grip, and turned to leave the room.

The room was still. No one moved. Vinnie stared out into space. The Pipe looked like a frozen Venus de Milo standing marble-hard in a darkened corner. Rocky remained in the middle of the room, his head dropped down. He felt like Jesus surrounded by mocking Roman soldiers and wondered if Gino or any of his thugs would spear him in the side.

Instead, he heard Gino say, "Pipe, show Rocky out."

And with that, Rocky Delmonico began his debt to the Lofaccio family.

4

It was 8 p.m., and Rocky was finally at peace. He was lying on his bed, smoking and taking it easy. After returning from his mother's doc, he showered off the day's sweat and stress and quickly grabbed something to eat. Then he hid his ass in his room for the rest of the evening.

What a day, Rocky thought. Missing out on a big-money match and attending the disastrous funeral. Which gets him into trouble with Gino and his nutcase mother. Then he comes home and gets colossal grief from *his* mother because he put off taking her to her appointment.

His mother was getting more demanding by the minute. When he returned from

Gino's, she was all dressed up. She was waiting in the kitchen, yelling at him like he was some twelve-year-old. Never mind that he was taking her crap with slap welts and spit stinging his face. The last thing he needed when he walked through the door was the old crab breaking his chops. Nothing worse could've topped off the day than him ending up in a waiting room filled with a menagerie of grumpy geezers waiting for their bogus doc visits. It was the proverbial icing on the cake.

He could only imagine what kind of payback he'd have to do for Gino. Over the years, he worked for Gino in various odd jobs: Chauffeuring Gino here and there, working at Gino's dance club as a bouncer and being an errand boy for Mrs. Lofaccio—all crap jobs. The bouncer gig was the worst. Wrestling with drunks after they got too cute with the dancers wasn't his idea of a future career track.

Shooting Bogies

But Rocky's size convinced Gino he was the perfect man for the job. And when you don't have a job and ask Gino for a gig, you take what you can get. Especially when it's Gino Lofaccio, not your typical career counselor, doing the job placement.

But he put all those meaningless jobs behind him a year ago when he hooked up with Howard Kinder. Howard was a godsend. Rocky enjoyed hustling money with his golf game. The last thing he wanted was to have to keep doing low-life jobs for Gino. But he knew his ass was now in a sling. God only knew what the little bastard was up to. He had to sweat out the next few days and wait. He should have told Gino the truth. Explain why he laughed like a crazy person when Mrs. Lofaccio jumped into her old man's grave. Gino would never have believed him. Thinking maybe he was trying to bullshit him. And forget Mrs. Lofaccio. She was probably rolling up her sleeves and getting ready to give him a beating no matter what. And how could he have possibly explained his behavior to Gino with Vinnie sitting in the room?

Better to plead guilty than to plead guilty with an explanation. Just like when you get a speeding ticket. And you go to court and say to the judge, 'Yes, your honor, I'm guilty, but I have an explanation.' The judge sits there and listens to your story. Then, after you're done, he slams down his gavel, declares you guilty, and whacks you with as hefty a fine as the original ticket. So, what does it matter explaining your guilt? You might as well take it on the chin and save time.

Of course, he knew about the Lofaccio tradition of jumping into open graves. Five years ago, he'd witnessed Gino's Aunt Toni swan diving into *her* husband's grave. That time, though, The Pipe had elbowed him and whispered, "Here she goes," so he was prepared. The Pipe also gave him a heads-up about Aunt Toni the night before the funeral. He told Rocky about some old-world ritual the Lofaccio widows do to stomp on spirits trying to get out of the casket. But today, with The Pipe hanging close to Gino on the other side of the gravesite, Rocky didn't have any heads-up. So when he saw the old biddy jump into the grave, Rocky started to laugh. It was good that Gino gave him that killer look, even though he knew he was immediately screwed. Getting the shit scared out of him was the only thing that could have made him stop.

Rocky's shrink called it an aberrant behavioral response. The doc was the only person in the world who knew about his condition, and Rocky planned to keep it that way. Even his mother didn't know. Rocky developed it during his year-long stint in Kuwait during the first Gulf War. It was part of the post-traumatic syndrome thing he was still dealing with. As the army shrink explained it, laughing like crazy was Rocky's way of dealing with the stress triggers of death.

He developed the condition after being assigned to drive an ambulance during the war. But his Commanding Officer quickly transferred him out of the unit because he was hauling the wounded into medical tents while laughing his head off. When he finished pushing a pencil as a Quartermaster's assistant and got discharged, the Army doc gave him a list of shrinks in his area.

Rocky found a guy he liked in Manhattan. The shrink was skinny, odd-looking, wore wire-rim glasses, and had long hair that fell to his shoulders. He looked like a folk-singing guitarist. Not exactly the Bellville, New Jersey type of guy Rocky was used to hanging with. In fact, the guy had no idea where Belleville, New Jersey was. That was perfect for Rocky, who wanted to keep his condition under wraps.

Shooting Bogies

So here he was, a chubby 34-year-old with a better-than-scratch golf handicap that he had been hustling over the years. And now he was making great money hustling golf matches with Howard Kinder. More money than he had ever made before. He didn't want anything to ruin or interfere with that relationship. Including whatever Gino had in store for him. Rocky looked up from his bed. His clock read 10 p.m.—time to put the day behind him.

5

The Woodland Crest Country Club was, without question, the prettiest piece of real estate in Belleville, New Jersey. With a clubhouse that sat on a bluff high above Bloomfield Avenue, it had idyllic views of the New York City skyline from almost every tee box on its golf course. Founded and incorporated as a golf club in 1895 by a group of local merchants, most of whom settled into Belleville after crossing the Atlantic from Ireland and Scotland, the club catered to a diverse membership, many not fitting the profile of the typical country club member. No question, very few members at Woodland Crest would ever be taken for the white shoe characters roaming the pages of *The Great Gatsby*. Instead, most of its 275 members started life in the more *Oliver Twist* mold: Scraping and hustling paychecks in the blue-collar neighborhoods of Belleville, Nutley, Lyndhurst, Queens, Brooklyn, and the Bronx and then morphing into shrewd entrepreneurs, savvy Wall Street traders, streetwise lawyers, and straight-talking doctors. No trust fund babies here.

It was a place where its members disdained inherited wealth. That attitude was a not-too-subtle slap at the blue blood clubs operating within an 8-iron of Woodland Crest, clubs who looked down their genteel, zinc oxide-coated noses at Woodland Crest's more proletariat-rooted membership. And it was precisely the kind of golf club that Howard Kinder, a former street kid from Brooklyn who made a fortune on Wall Street, wanted to belong to and finally joined when he moved into the northern New Jersey area.

When Kinder was 12, he came home one spring afternoon holding his latest report card with five gold stars. He again made the honor roll at P.S. 122 in Bay Ridge, Brooklyn, and was eager to get the $1.25 (.25 for each gold star) his father had promised him. Sitting outside the house that his mother, father, and younger brother shared with his paternal grandparents were two police cars and an ambulance. As he walked closer to his home, he could hear his mother wailing and sobbing uncontrollably. Kinder was terrified by the scene. As the young lad walked up the stoop, a police officer came through the front door of his house and quietly turned little Howard towards his squad car.

He asked Howard to get into the car's front seat. As they drove around the neighborhood, the police officer gently told Howard that his father had suddenly died of a heart attack at work. Patrolman Phillip

Shooting Bogies

Desano told him he was now the man of the house and needed to look after his mother and brother from here on in. Not wanting to bring the boy back to the house, Desano took Howard to Coney Island, where they spent the rest of the afternoon playing arcade games and eating hot dogs and ice cream.

Later that summer, Howard, his mother, and his brother moved out of his grandparents' house. Grandpa Kinder and Howard's mother always argued so the family found a basement apartment in the Flatbush section of Brooklyn. It was here that Howard would start life anew: a new neighborhood, new friends, and, most importantly, a new school called Erasmus Hall High School, one of the best high schools in New York City at that time.

While at first "Howard the whiz kid" floundered in school, not finding anything particularly important or exciting after his father's death, he soon committed to the Erasmus Hall education. He found his motivation to succeed during his sophomore through senior years. When graduation came, Howard had several full scholarships and eventually selected Harvard as his school of choice. After graduating from Harvard with a business degree, Howard took a job with Crenshaw Securities, a New York-based international banking firm (he had worked part-time summer jobs there, in addition to a job as a mower at Brooklyn's Dyker Beach Golf Course) and rose quickly through Crenshaw's ranks to become one of their top investment bankers.

After 15 years with Crenshaw, on the morning of September 11, 2001, Howard was enjoying a late dinner halfway around the world in Café Deco, a hip restaurant in Hong Kong's fashionable Victoria Peak section. Howard and his wife Judy had moved

Shooting Bogies

there just the year before, overseeing Crenshaw's Pacific Rim operations. The job was considered a stepping-stone to the top position of Crenshaw Securities. At 39, Howard was on the fast track to become the youngest Chairman in Crenshaw's history.

Howard immediately left his dinner companions when news of the attack on the twin towers swept through the Café Deco. He headed for his penthouse condo a few blocks away. As he watched the tragedy unfold with Judy, all he could think of was his mother in Brooklyn and, more importantly, his younger brother David. David Kinder was a New York City police officer based in the Fifth Precinct in lower Manhattan. Howard knew that if David was on duty today, he would be in the thick of the attack.

As he watched the towers fall, Howard got a knot in his stomach and a sense that David was in harm's way. With all the havoc going on in New York City, it was impossible to place a telephone call to his mother or his brother, making Howard's urgency to find out anything even more frustrating. It wasn't until Thursday, September 13, before Howard learned his brother was indeed missing. It took another month before David's death was confirmed.

A week after David's memorial service, Howard decided he no longer wanted to be halfway around the world from his roots. He decided to ask Crenshaw for a transfer back to New York. He understood that a transfer meant he was stepping off the fast track, a possibility that both he and Judy accepted.

When he met with Jack Berke, the chairman of Crenshaw Securities, his proposal was met with open hostility, not only from Jack but also from several members of Crenshaw's board. They accused him of being selfish, self-centered, and not acting in the company's best interests. They wouldn't hear of him leaving Hong Kong and offered no alternatives or options.

Stunned by his boss' reaction, Howard returned to Crenshaw's offices the next day and quit. He was a 39-year-old multi-millionaire and fully understood how fragile life could be. With the early death of his dad and the sudden tragedy of his younger brother, getting to the top of Crenshaw just wasn't important to him anymore. He decided to take some time off, do some consulting, day trade to keep his hand in the Wall Street game and join Woodland Crest to work on his golf game.

One late April day in the early spring of 2002, Howard was hitting golf balls at the Lodi Park Golf Driving Range in Lodi, New Jersey. He was still waiting to hear if he was accepted as a member of Woodland Crest. Hitting golf balls in the stall beside him was a funny-looking, roly-poly man. The man was dressed all in black and, despite his awkward size, had the smoothest golf swing Howard had ever seen. But what got Howard's attention was that this guy was placing $50 bets on the placements of his shots with a young guy standing behind him. By the time the session ended, Junior had handed over more than $500 to this oversized golf hustler. Howard was enjoying every minute of watching the hustle take place. When it was over, the hustler noticed Howard's interest and asked if he was looking for action.

"No thanks," Howard laughed, not wanting to be this guy's next victim.

"Then how about a lesson?" the hustler asked. "I hate to see a guy swing as badly as you do. I can fix that awkward swing of yours."

Howard was amused at the hustle but negotiated a $50 half-hour lesson on a lark. Howard knew he had found his golf muse twenty minutes into the lesson. Although the guy was rough around the edges, Howard connected to his street ethic. The hustler's grittiness reminded Howard of his brother. More importantly, he saw that Rocky knew golf technique. They agreed to meet the following Wednesday and subsequent Wednesdays after that.

It was on the Lodi Park Golf Driving Range and the post-lesson calamari dinners they shared at the Il Fornaio restaurant in Belleville that Howard Kinder, a Brooklyn-born, Wall Street multi-millionaire, became fast friends with Rocky Delmonico, a Belleville-born golf hustler. Both would proudly say it would be a marriage born in golf heaven.

The high point of their friendship that first year was Woodland Crest's most prestigious member-guest event in early October. It was created by a past member named Xavier Osborne. It was an event to promote Woodland Crest to new member prospects wishing to join the following year. Over the years, the X.O., as members called it, evolved into a serious two-day money tournament where the winning member-guest twosome could pocket $10,000-$15,000 to split. Not a bad payday for a couple of country club amateur hacks. The savvy club member knew that to have a shot at first-place winnings, you needed to invite a guest with a great game and calm nerves while playing for serious money.

Being a golf hustler, Rocky had no problem playing in money matches. He'd been playing golf since he was ten, his Uncle Tony turning him onto the game on the local Essex County courses. But what Rocky really liked to do when he was a kid was practice, practice, and more practice. Rocky spent winter, spring, fall, and summer days in Uncle Tony's garage down the street on Montague, hitting thousands of golf balls into a net hung from a wooden beam. Rocky found the repetitive routine of swinging a golf club in Uncle

Shooting Bogies

Tony's garage calming *and* a world he could go where nobody called him fat.

You could say Rocky found Nirvana in a musty, drafty garage. Uncle Tony had set up a small homemade putting contraption in the garage, too. Here, Rocky deftly honed his putting skills morning, noon, and night. By the time Rocky was 13, he was playing for money—his Uncle Tony backing his game against golfers twice his age. And while he played country club courses now and then as he grew into an adult, he mostly played and made his living on public courses in New Jersey, Pennsylvania, New York, Florida, and Myrtle Beach.

While his real handicap was now a +2, meaning he regularly played courses at two under par, he missed enough putts to shoot bogeys when the hole was lost, or it didn't count. He deliberately missed these putts to maintain a four handicap. By doing so, he had a cushion of 6 strokes against any competitor, quite an advantage through a regular round of 18 holes. Such tactics are the tools of a golf hustler.

But the genius behind Rocky's golf hustle wasn't his golf prowess. Rocky's real hustle was the way he looked and spoke. Standing just a shade under six feet and a body size that leaned into corpulence, Rocky was prematurely bald, often wore glasses (when he wasn't wearing his contacts) and had an aura of impending doom about him. To a stranger, Rocky looked like an out-of-shape misshapen geek. And if his appearance wasn't enough for anyone to think he was going nowhere, Rocky's ride made him look like a loser. He drove a very old Ford Econoline van painted in gray primer. For some reason, a small stovepipe came through the roof, and the van was missing three hubcaps. It looked like it had been rescued from a junkyard. At any glance, first or otherwise, he was not what someone would call a typical-looking golfer.

Shooting Bogies

Rocky was also blessed with what athletes call great hands. They were oversized, robust, yet highly touch-sensitive, especially around or on the greens. He would say he could feel the dimples on the golf ball on impact, feeling the ball slip off the face of the club and start its furious rotation to Rocky's intended target. He attributed his highly sensitive hands to his meticulously soft putting stroke. He often likened putting to the velvety, precise action of shooting pool.

When the dust cleared after their first X.O. tournament, Howard and Rocky pocketed nearly $10,000 each. Not only had they won first place in the X.O., which had brought them $7,500 each, but they also won numerous side bets against other competing twosomes.

Howard enjoyed being with Rocky. And while Howard had moved on from Brooklyn to amass a fortune on Wall Street and accumulated the trappings of a wealthy lifestyle, underneath the high-priced suits, the luxury homes, the sports cars, the Swiss watches, home theaters, fine wines, cigars, and jet-set vacations, Howard was still a street kid from Brooklyn. And he loved nothing better than hanging with other street guys.

As they walked to their cars in Woodland Crest's parking lot after a raucous post-tournament party toasting Howard and Rocky's X.O. win, Howard made Rocky an offer that Rocky couldn't refuse.

"Rocky," Howard began, "we've had a great ride this year since we first met in Lodi."

"Yeah, it's been fun," Rocky answered, throwing his clubs into the back of his van.

"I want to do something that will make us both happy," Howard said. "I want you to stop doing what you just did."

"What did I just do?" Rocky asked.

"You threw your clubs into your van."

"So?"

"Well, I don't want you to do that anymore," Howard said.

"What's that?"

"I want to sponsor you for membership in Woodland Crest," Howard announced. "You can store your clubs there."

"Can't afford it, Howard," Rocky said. "The money I make hustling and working at the range doesn't come close to the fees and dues of a country club membership."

"But you're not buying it, Rocky, I am," Howard said.

"Can't accept it, Howard."

"Yes, you can."

"No, I can't," Rocky shot back.

"It's already done," Howard said, smiling. "And don't worry about what you can and can't afford. I will be setting up matches that will generate big paydays."

And with that, Howard set in motion the application process for having Mr. Rocco Aloysious Delmonico become a full-fledged member of the Woodland Crest Golf Club. By March of the following year, Rocky was admitted under the sponsorship of Howard Kinder and five other members.

6

Meeting Howard was the best thing that ever happened to Rocky. Howard treated him like an equal, introduced him to many interesting people at the club, and, most importantly, set up numerous golf matches that generated more money for Rocky than he had ever dreamed of. Before meeting Howard, Rocky's life was a mixture of doing all sorts of odd jobs for Gino while also making a decent living on the public golf courses and at the golf range in Lodi. The trouble was that while Rocky's winnings on the golf course far surpassed anything he made with Gino, he needed more matches to make his golf hustling sustainable. Meeting Howard changed all that.

With Howard setting things up, Rocky stayed busy making money hustling golf, not only at Woodland Crest but at numerous golf clubs in northern, central, or southern New Jersey, and clubs in Boston, Vegas, Virginia, Miami, Dallas, Los Angeles, Scottsdale, and San Francisco. Howard had even set up a match at the Beijing Golf Club, a thirty-minute drive from China's capital. Howard knew people in just about every city in the world. People with lots of money. People who loved golf and enjoyed playing for big money. Rocky was happy to oblige their competitive streak and usually came home a winner. There were matches, however, when Howard would give him the high sign to take a dive and intentionally lose a game. These rounds were thrown to either set up a future match with more considerable action or simply because Howard wanted to lose for some business angle.

Shooting Bogies

In addition to making great money, which Rocky knew was chump change to Howard, Rocky was also beginning to distance himself from Gino Lofaccio and his bullshit jobs. His biggest concern was keeping Gino and his crew in the dark about all the action he was winning with Howard. He was sure that if Gino caught wind of his earnings with Howard, Gino, being the prick that he was, would want in. And the last thing Rocky wanted was for Howard to get mixed up with Gino and his boys. He would do anything to make sure that would never happen.

Besides the money, Rocky viewed his friendship with Howard as a new beginning. A "good luck" road that he had never had the fortune to walk down before. Ever since he was a kid, Rocky sensed good luck was for everybody else and that if bad things were to happen, they would indeed happen to him. He was convinced he was born under a bad sign and that bad luck would shadow him forever. As he learned, bad luck was a tradition in the Delmonico family. And it was at the root of Rocky's deep-seated superstitions.

"Look at all the tragedies in our family," his mother often cried to young Rocky. "Tell me our family isn't cursed! Just look around. Look around!"

His mother, grandmother, and aunts' fatalistic attitude seeped into young Rocky's skin. And it didn't stop there. Every room in Rocky's house had a shrine to ward off the ever-intrusive "evil eye" lurking everywhere. The St. Jude shrine was in Renata's room. A St. Christopher altar was in the kitchen. St. John the Baptist was in his mother's room. And the Virgin Mary and the blessed Jesus were in his room, which doubled as the living room. Young Rocky was given a new religious talisman every year through elementary school, seemingly to protect him from evil tidings. There were a variety of lucky charms his mother gave him. His favorites were the first-grade rabbit's foot, the third-grade Madonna patch sewn into his pants pocket, and the eighth-grade glass amulet filled with holy water from some far-off place in Portugal. And to batten down the hatches against impending doom, every Delmonico adult woman also practiced some form of witchcraft.

Rocky was first introduced to his family's witchcraft when he was eight years old, and his maternal grandmother came for a summer visit from Yugoslavia. She stayed four weeks, and during that month, Rocky was introduced to bizarre spiritual beliefs and witchcraft rituals. Weird stuff beyond his Catholic school teachings. They left indelible impressions on him that he would carry through his life. His grandmother even taught him that his surname was a possible omen to ruin, a cautionary revelation that would further shatter his confidence, self-worth, and esteem.

"Little Rocco, you must be careful throughout your life," Grandma counseled in a thick Slavic accent. "Even your last name is cursed. Look here."

As they sat in the small dark kitchen on a summer evening, little Rocky stared in wide-eyed wonder as the musty old woman, dressed head to toe in black, with a wrinkly face, yellow teeth, and wet eyes, printed out his last name on a piece of stark white paper:

D-E-L-M-O-N-I-C-O.

"Now, Rocco, see what your name spells without the L," she said. And with that, she placed a bent right index finger over the L.

"Do you see, Rocco, what it spells?"

Rocky had to shift high in the kitchen chair to look around her finger as he made out the letters, which now read:

D-E-M-O-N-I-C-O.
"Do you know what these letters mean, Rocco?" she asked again. And with that, she went on to erase the last three letters of his name and left only these:

D-E-M-O-N

When Rocky shook his head no, the little woman explained what a demon was and that his last name was "infested" with the devil.

"Be careful, little Rocco," she counseled. "You have bad omens attached to you. Omens brought on to you by your father's name."

She told him that he must be cautious at all times.

Vigilant when he walks down a quiet street.

Wary of anyone's intentions who were outside the family.

Alert for any impending disasters.

She warned him of demons disguised as black dogs.

"You can tell they are demons by their flaming eyes," she cautioned.

She told him about child stealers, bogeymen, and night raiders who came in the dead of night, usually around midnight, and ate children while they slept. She cautioned Rocky about witches disguised as beautiful women who trick little children into going with them. And witches disguised as cats or birds. She especially advised Rocky never to walk alone in forests because of the danger of being a victim of demonic elves or giants who prowl among the trees searching for children.

Little Rocco stared back at her, gripped by fear. No one had ever spoken to him like this before. He wondered if these things this old woman was telling him were true or were fantasy stories made up to scare him. Much like the stories the older kids on his block would tell. He wondered where anything resembling a forest in Belleville, New Jersey, might be except for the nearby golf course. But Rocky dared not utter a word. He dared not ask a question. He just stared at the piece of paper on the kitchen table that read D-E-M-O-N and became frightened that he would have to go to sleep that night.

7

As Rocky stood over his 4-foot par putt on the 18th green at the Woodland Crest Country Club, all he was thinking was stroking the ball with as delicate a touch as he could muster. Rocky could drain 4-foot putts in his sleep. But Woodland Crest's 18th green was lightning-fast, the most unforgiving green on the course, and any putt from above the hole could be the beginning of a significant scorecard disaster. Even a delicate stroke could turn into a 20-foot comeback attempt if the ball didn't drop into the hole. The green was especially fast and nasty today. Howard had tipped Tony the groundskeeper a new Franklin to double roll the green to make it faster. Just in case Oliver and Mark

Shooting Bogies

Kang, Rocky's and Howard's opponents, made the match a close contest.

His approach shot on this 435-yard par-4 was exactly how Rocky wanted it. The ball landed about twenty yards short of the green, bounded up, and after a couple of bounces, settled on the green for what was to be an easy below-the-hole birdie attempt. But Rocky decided to be more aggressive with the birdie putt than he should have, sending the ball well past the cup. With all the Nassaus already won and $9,000 waiting to be split between himself and Howard, Rocky threw caution to the wind and went hard at the birdie. And why not? Making the birdie putt would have earned Rocky and Howard another grand each.

Plus, the Kangs were looking for more action. This after they lost the match on 16. They wanted to play 17 and 18 for $500 a man, with birdies worth a g-note. Howard and Rocky agreed and promptly won 17.

Now, on 18, the Kang brothers had already made par. But instead of playing the first putt cautiously, getting the par, calling the hole a draw, and getting off the course, Rocky got cute. He was now looking at bogeying the hole. Rocky gave a rat's ass about the money. After all, walking away with $4,000 for four hours of work was a good day. And Howard, bless his heart, who already was in his pocket with a bogey on 18, couldn't care less. But it was the principle of the thing. Rocky wanted the putt. If for no other reason than to put an exclamation point on the match, which would make up for his stressful meeting with Gino.

Earlier that Saturday, word of the match had spread through the men's locker room. Everyone knew Rocky and Howard were to play for some serious money. And in the clubby world of country club golf, asking just how much was déclassé. But with serious action whispering through the club, small crowds would spontaneously appear on a fairway or around a green. Throughout the match, Rocky noticed many club members pulling aside or motioning for an update from Ian, his caddy. After winning the match on 16, Ian was signaling the thumbs up. Now, two dozen golfers were milling around the 18th green as Rocky studied the putt's line. Rocky had his golf-playing reputation rolling on this putt, too.

Not three weeks ago, he had a similar putt. The putt broke three inches right to left. That last time, he had drained it with no problem. He knew precisely how the putt was to be played, but what bothered Rocky today was a rogue ball mark that was part of the putting line. He was confident the mark would influence the ball's line, especially with the ball moving at such a slow speed. It was a blemish made and not repaired by a hacker who played in a corporate outing the day before.

Rocky stood over the ball and stroked. As the ball rolled over the mark, it did what Rocky feared. It never took the break because the mark misdirected its course. Instead, the ball stayed out to the right and came to rest just a half-inch off the hole. As a chorus of oohs and groans rose from the crowd, Rocky quickly tapped in for the bogey to lose the hole. He collected the ball from the cup, stood up, and shook hands with the smiling and bowing Kangs. He flipped his putter to Ian and headed to the clubhouse.

After eating a chicken salad sandwich, a post-match ritual he followed after winning a golf match, Rocky was hanging out in the club's Men's Grill playing Hold 'em with some members. With a penchant for counting cards, Rocky was up another grand and was looking at a big pot when his cell phone rang.

Rocky noticed it was Howard calling. Howard had left the club earlier to drive the Kangs back to the airport. Rocky would have let the call go into voice mail if anyone else called during his card playing, but not Howard.

"Rocky, great news, man," Howard said, his voice underscored with enthusiasm.

"What's up, Howard?" Rocky asked as he saw a raise by throwing a $100 chip into the middle of the table.

"We've got a new match set up against The Kids in a couple of weeks," Howard offered. "They want to play for $10,000 a hole, and they're willing to play you as a 6-handicap."

"Where are we playing?" Rocky asked, tossing in another $100 chip to meet the raiser again, wondering if this old guy wearing a faded Members Only jacket across from him was bluffing because he was on the phone.

"Vegas, Memorial Day weekend. The course still to be determined."

Rocky thought about his upcoming meeting with Gino and wondered if what that little prick wanted would interfere with the match.

"Works for me, Howard. Set it up."

"Great, Rocky. We'll have a blast and take The Kids to the cleaners. I told them you needed the 6-handicap because you haven't played much lately.

"Way to go, Howard. Catch you later."

Rocky saw that everyone at the table was showing their cards. The old pain in the ass who was raising showed kings up. That beat everyone else except Rocky, who flipped over aces up. As Rocky leaned over the table to hug in his winnings, he thought he was on a good luck roll—except for the humiliating few minutes in Gino's basement the previous Thursday. Though he did escape without a scratch. Whatever bullshit job Gino was planning for him, he would do it in one piece. He cleaned out a couple of pigeons for four long ones this morning. And he was a few grand up playing poker. Not a bad roll, he thought, although the memory of that poorly repaired ball mark that caused him to bogey 18 was tempering his joy.

As Rocky drove home from the club $6,500 richer than the morning, his winnings at the poker table almost matching his day's golf earnings, he considered playing The Kids. The Kids were a couple of young high-tech turks based in Seattle who made a fortune developing online software. Howard met The Kids through a deal Crenshaw Securities made with their company. He nicknamed them The Kids because they were precisely that: A couple of twenty-somethings worth a billion after selling to a larger company. Between running the show under the new company, The Kids spent their free time pissing away money gambling on everything, including their shitty golf games. But losing money was of no consequence to The

Kids. Often, they just laughed it off. They had amassed such a fortune that their losses were covered just by the interest generated from their principal. In addition to enjoying taking their money, Rocky liked playing golf with The Kids because they were such fun-loving, happy-go-lucky guys. They probably never thought about bad omens. Always positive. No demons, bogeymen, or Gino's hovering over their shoulders. Not a care in the world. It would have been nice to grow up like that. Maybe his next life, Rocky thought.

8

Rocky spent all day Monday doing a variety of chores and running errands. He washed the dishes. Took his mother grocery shopping. And he mowed the backyard. It seemed that no matter what, his mother always had a long list of things for him to do around the house. Ninety-nine percent of the time the chores were all bullshit stuff to keep him around. But they were part of the trade-off of living with his mother. Rocky wasn't sure exactly when he knew he would never move out of his mother's house. It just evolved. But it wasn't all bad. He often found refuge when he escaped to the upstairs apartment he moved into when he returned home from Kuwait.

In some ways, Rocky felt he had become a victim of circumstances well beyond his control. First, his old man died when he was 10. And then, a couple of years later, Renata drowned. That left Rocky alone with his mother, and except for his time in the Army, Rocky never was away from Montague Street for any length of time. His mother's house was long ago paid off. His father's life insurance covered that, so there was no rent or mortgage. The living expenses were property taxes, food, electricity, water, and heat. The electric and heating costs were already at rock bottom. Several years ago, Rocky paid off one of Gino's boys, Tony "Circuits" Marrone, to come to the house to reconfigure the electric meters. Tony Circuits was an electric utility guy from New York City who was a whiz at cheating electric companies, gas companies, digital satellite companies, cable companies, and any company that beamed something electric, digital or otherwise into your house. For $300, Tony would come in and "fix" your home and save you hundreds of dollars a year. If you bought Tony's $500 deluxe package, Tony Circuits would get you HBO, the NFL Network, and a slew of other premium cable channels all on the arm.

And for a grand, Tony would deliver all those services, then back the odometer on not one but two of your cars—any car, any odometer, analog or digital. Nothing was a challenge for Tony. He was a genius, and Gino loved using him on jobs that required his services.

As far as food costs were concerned, Rocky had taken care of that, too. His mother wasn't a big eater, but Rocky loved eating steak several nights a week. Rocky had a friend named Sal who worked in the meat department at the local ShopRite. Sal would give him great deals on steaks, often two for the price of one. All Rocky had to do was invite the guy to the club for a few rounds of golf every summer. Rocky often hustled Sal out of $100 during the rounds, which was just about what it cost Rocky in guest fees. But Sal didn't seem to mind being hustled. He enjoyed playing with Rocky at the local country club. When Rocky added it all up, in exchange for the errands and chores and taking his mother to endless doctor's appointments, Rocky had a great deal living in his mother's house.

It was 5 p.m., and he was hanging out in the second-floor apartment when his cell phone rang.

"Rocky, it's The Pipe. How you doin"?

"Doin' good today, Pipe. What's up."

"Just callin' to remind you of your meeting with Gino tonight."

"I'll be there, Pipe."

"Don't screw around, Rocky. Be there early even if he told you to be there at 9. Gino likes it when people come early. Be there at 8:30."

Shooting Bogies

"I got it, Pipe. I'll be there early."

"Don't forget. We'll be at Maximus. See you there."

"See you later, Pipe."

From the outside, Maximus was an ornate building oddly neighbored by a junkyard, a scrap metal factory, and a recycling facility. It was located in an industrial part of Newark that would never see 21st-century urban reconstruction, new housing development, or any other government program trying to do good for Newark's citizenry. The only redevelopment the area had seen was the meticulously paved access road leading to Maximus's front door. Gino had a guy on the payroll who worked for the County and got him to pull strings to resurface the street. Gino wanted to avoid any of his customers driving over potholes and bumps when they came to his club. The exterior of Maximus had a façade that replicated a Roman palace. Corinthian columns framed the massive gold door entryway. Bas reliefs of grapes, cherubs, Roman soldiers, tigers, and female nudes adorned Maximus' elaborate entrance. High-quality Carrara marble imported from Italy formed the steps and hallway, all glistening under hot-white klieg lights. All this brought a touch of Las Vegas to a gloomy, rundown industrial neighborhood. The building looked like a single glistening white front tooth set amongst a row of tetracycline gray teeth.

Standing guard in front of this elaborate Roman entrance was the imposing figure of Vinnie Bellomo. Dressed in his black, shiny suit and reeking of the low-level New Jersey hood that he was, Vinnie doubled as Maximus' box office clerk and door bouncer. Every night Maximus was open, Vinnie would often hold a wad of cash, adding up to $20,000 or more at any moment. That's how popular Maximus and its lap-dancing girls were. Gino set the Maximus admission price

Shooting Bogies

at $200 a man. At this price, he said, we'll keep the "phony moolinyan gangstas and the rowdy college assholes out and attract respectable businesspeople." Gino, no doubt, was into target marketing.

Gino told Rocky: "For two C-notes, the tie and suit guys get three drinks, safe parking, and the chance to hound the best dancers this side of Las Vegas."

And the armada of Ferraris, Lambos, Lexuses, and Beemers that pulled up to the front door confirmed Gino's vision. Indeed, almost all of Maximus' customers were financial service or Wall Street guys who either worked on Broad Street in Newark, drove up from their offices in Jersey City, or came across the river from New York City. And Gino knew these guys were very particular about their cars, many having stronger feelings for their wheels than their girlfriends or wives. That's why he paid a few long ones in bribes to get the access road repaved. Then, he purchased a building across the street from Maximus to convert it into a valet parking garage.

When Rocky arrived at 8:30, Maximus was already jumping. The street backed up with shiny, late-model cars waiting to be parked. Over the weekend, the New Jersey Devils had advanced into the final conference round, and game 1 of the series was being played tonight. In addition to three drinks, safe valet parking, and dancing girls, Maximus' customers would be treated to large-screen plasma TVs showing a New Jersey Devils-New York Rangers conference game. What more could a Wall Street guy ask for?

Rocky swung his primer gray van around the valet line of serious-money rides. He parked in the employee lot in the back, a place that was pitted, potholed, and bumpy. He knocked on the back door and again was greeted by The Pipe, who led him downstairs to Gino's office. Although Rocky had been in

Gino's club office many times before, Rocky felt a dread that he was re-living his Thursday afternoon exploit. He had no idea what the little hump had in mind for him to make things "right," and the situation's uncertainty made him nervous.

Sitting in a darkened corner was the ubiquitous Mrs. Lofaccio, her haunting, menacing presence giving Rocky the chills. She was like that scary black bird in a poem Rocky had to read in high school English class. A big black bird that represented death. Rocky couldn't sleep for three days after reading that poem. He couldn't square how Gino allowed his mother to work at a gentlemen's club. When Rocky worked the Maximus floor a few summers ago, it wasn't unusual to see Mrs. Lofaccio walking the club while girls danced away on the stage or performed gyrating lap dances on top of the suits.

"Sit down, Rocky," Gino said, smiling up a storm as if he was receiving a long-lost buddy. "What can I get you to drink? Daniels? Scotch? Vodka? What'll it be?"

"Nothing, Gino, I'm fine," Rocky said, as he nervously fingered his good-luck, holy water amulet tucked safely in his jacket pocket.

Rocky hadn't been in this office in quite some time. The place was soundproofed up the wazoo, so the loud, thumping music blaring upstairs in Maximus's mirrored main room was blocked out. Gino also had Tony Circuits debug the office, installing high-tech, state-of-the-art sensors to monitor whether anyone, law enforcement or otherwise, planted listening devices in the room. Where Tony installed these devices was anybody's guess.

"So Rocky, I heard you had a nice score over the weekend at that fancy Woodland Crest," Gino said as he sat at his desk. "I know all about this Kinder guy you play golf with, Rocky. It seems you and him have a nice thing going."

Rocky was stunned that Gino knew about his golf hustles with Howard, yet at the same time, he wasn't at all surprised. He tried not to show his surprise but knew he was failing miserably. It seemed like the little hump knew almost everything around the neighborhood.

"You don't like that, Rocky?" Gino smiled smugly. "Me knowing about your golf? I've known for quite some time that you were a "money-hustling" golfer. Good for you, Rocky. Good for you."

Rocky could not guess who may have tipped off Gino about his golf hustle.

Gino sensed what Rocky was thinking.

"You know Johnny Rhodes?"

"Yeah, Gino, he's a sometime bartender at Woodland Crest. Works the Men's Grill there", Rocky said.

"Well, he works for me too. Part-time stuff. Like he does at Woodland Crest. Good guy," Gino said. "That's how I know how good you are at swinging a golf club, plus all the money you're making. This little favor you owe my mother and me also involves swinging a golf club. How about that, Rocky?" We have here what they call a perfect fit. I planned to ask you to help me, Rocky. But after last week, I'm no longer asking. Understand, Rocky?"

Rocky shifted nervously in his seat. He felt his blood pressure rising again, much like he felt it spike in Gino's basement on Thursday. Rocky thought that Gino was ordering a hit, with Rocky using a 5-iron over somebody's skull.

"Here's the deal," Gino said, getting up from his chair, a magazine grasped tightly in his hands and coming around the desk. "You know this guy, Rocky?" Gino asked as he flipped Rocky a copy of *New Jersey Inc.* magazine.

Rocky looked at the magazine. On the cover was a guy named Pincus Bogalinsky. The tanned Bogalinsky stood on a golf course, smiling into the camera. He wore a powder-blue Versace golf shirt and was sporting an elaborate, two-dial, diamond-studded wristwatch worth over $100,000. Bogalinky's highly bleached white teeth radiated from the cover. It was a smile that Rocky figured set him back another 25K. And parked majestically behind him was a steel blue Bentley Continental GTC, a car valued, Rocky estimated, at more than 225K.

The title on the magazine cover read: "New Jersey's CEO of the Year: How Pincus Bogalinsky Turned Around Fair Play."

"Ever hear of him, Rocky?" Gino asked, interrupting Rocky's focus on the magazine cover.

"No, Gino, I don't know him," Rocky said. "Though I know Fair Play. It's one of the top golf courses in New Jersey. A beautiful course. Very well-maintained. Very exclusive membership, something like 350K to join. The membership is made up of rich Wall Street guys mainly."

"Like to play there sometime, Rocky?"

"Sure, Gino, that would be fun."

"Well," Gino said, smiling, hopping off his desk and approaching Rocky, cradling Rocky's face.

"You'll have plenty of opportunities to do just that," Gino said, smiling and staring straight into Rocky's eyes. "Let me be the first to congratulate you. As of now, Rocky, you are the new head golf pro at Fair Play!"

9

Rocky's head began to throb. It took him about two minutes to process what Gino had said. He couldn't believe what he heard: Him, Rocky, being the new golf pro at the Fair Play Country Club in Wellington, New Jersey. The last thing Rocky wanted or needed was a full-time job anywhere, including on a golf course. Things were working out just fine with Howard. Just because he was a scratch golfer didn't mean he wanted to spend every day around a golf course. Rocky enjoyed just hanging out, too. Messing around in New York every week after seeing his shrink. And just plain loafing around the house in his raggy clothes. Having a full-time job was just not for him.

"Aren't you excited?" Rocky heard Gino ask.

"Well, Gino," Rocky said, "I really wasn't looking for a full-time job right now."

"Maybe not," Gino responded. "But you do want to make amends, don't you, for your behavior at my father's funeral last week?"

"Yes, Gino, I do."

"Well, Rocky, accepting this job is your amends," Gino said in a cold and calculating tone that Rocky knew better than to argue with. He quickly realized it was time to get with Gino's program, suddenly accepting there was no possible way out of *not* taking the job. He was still trying to figure out how agreeing to this job would make amends, but he was confident Gino would tell him why. While he knew he had to atone for his actions last week, he underestimated how deeply he pissed off Gino and his crazy mother.

"Thank you, Gino," Rocky blurted out. "I'll do my best, though I don't know the first thing about being a golf pro."

Shooting Bogies

"Being a fucking golf pro is the least of what I want you to do at Fair Play," Gino revealed. "Rocky, I want you to be my eyes and ears there. I want you to earn Bogalinsky's trust. Keep your ear to the ground. Find out what is up his sleeve. I want to buy that place, Rocky. I don't give a shit about a golf course, either. I can put a ton of condos on that shitty course. I wanna develop there. Less than an hour's drive from AC and the beach. It's a goddam condo goldmine for Chrissakes, and I want it to be mine."

Rocky thought about what Gino was saying. Southern New Jersey real estate prices had gone through the roof since they built the first casinos in Atlantic City in the late 70s. The open expanses of land that once supported tomato and vegetable farms and brush pines were now underneath an explosion of sprawling condo and house developments. Southern New Jersey around Atlantic City was the state's fastest growing area, a sizable chunk coming from all the old, taillight-blinking geezers moving down there from the northern New Jersey counties. But Rocky was still confused about his role in Gino's plans.

"I'm still not sure how I can help. Or what exactly do you want me to do"? Rocky asked.

"Rocky, are you a moron or what?" Gino screamed. "I just told you what I want you to do. Let me give it to you in black and white. This guy took over the course last year. He messed up a real estate deal I was getting this close to making happen. Came in with a ridiculous price at the last minute, well below my bid. But his Wall Street friends finagled a deal with the bankers and the State of New Jersey assholes who held title to the place. Those rat bastards. They are worse than the moolinyans. I don't like to lose, and this guy screwed me royally. But he doesn't own the place yet. He has a lease arrangement with an option to buy. Has until July 15, less than two and a half months away, to exercise the buy option. I don't want this prick to do that. It will go to auction if he doesn't pick up the option. If the place goes to auction, I win. Don't ask how. I need to know what he's thinking and whether he will buy it. It's time to get this land, Rocky. I don't want to wait any longer."

Rocky was trying to absorb everything Gino was saying. Gino was looking to score a land grab. Somehow, he got screwed out of a deal. Now he wants revenge and the land back. He needs me as his point man down there. He wants me to rat out this guy's intentions. How would all this play? And if Bogalinsky opts to buy? What then? Rocky wanted to avoid asking those end-game questions. I'm getting deeper into Gino's business, Rocky thought. More than I ever wanted to be. More than just being a club bouncer, a chauffeur for Mrs. Lofaccio, or a low-level gofer like The Pipe.

"The general manager of Fair Play is Pete Malone," Gino said, interrupting Rocky's thoughts. "Pete's working for us. At first, he didn't want to, but he came around fast after we showed him photographs of him going into a Motel Six with a high school senior. Not good for him if the wife and kids find out. He knows you'll be down soon and working for us. And you want to know what the good news is, Rocky?"

"What's that, Gino?"

"You'll be on the books for 100Gs. You'll be legit. And this guy Bogalinky is a real golf nut. Though from what I've heard, he sucks. Most of the time, you'll be working on this douchebag's golf game. You'll have it made, Rocky. You start June 1, just like a real job. That doesn't give us much time to determine what this asshole is up to."

"What happened to the current pro?" Rocky asked.

Shooting Bogies

"He's still there, but he's going away soon. But don't ask any more questions," Gino said. "You just worry about getting down there and cozying up to Bogalinsky. You'll be like what the Arabs call my little sleeper cell. Gino Lofaccio's one-person sleeper cell at Fair Play. All I need for you to do is keep an eye on this scumbag until July 15. Then we're done. You can go back to your golf hustles with Kinder after that. In the meantime, you are to listen for anything that tips Bogalinsky's hand on whether he's buying this place. And if you hear of anything, you let me know that minute. Understand, Rocky?"

"Yeah, Gino, I got it. But how long do you figure I gotta be down there, Gino?" Rocky asked, sensing he was pushing it with Gino now. "I got my mother and all, Gino." Rocky liked to play the momma's boy card, especially with Gino, who was, at heart, a momma's boy, too.

"Rocky, for Chrissakes, don't you listen? By July 14, we'll know where he stands and where we stand," Gino said. "And the only thing you need to worry about is finding out what his plans are. Nothing more, nothing less. If anybody asks you about anything else, you don't say nothing. You didn't hear nothing. You didn't see nothing. You got that, Rocky?"

"I understand, Gino," Rocky said, knowing that seeing, hearing, and saying nothing was crucial when you got involved with Gino Lofaccio.

"That's it for now," Gino said. Vinnie will call you in a week to go over the details. "Don't screw this up, Rocky, you hear?"

"I got it, Gino," Rocky said. "You can count on me."

When Rocky's grandmother visited during that fateful summer when she told him the devil possessed his name, she staged an incense-burning ceremony at 4 p.m. every afternoon. Little Rocky watched in wonder as she carefully spooned two teaspoons of a black powdery substance into a silver container that Rocky thought looked like a magical genie vase. After delicately tamping down the black incense in the bowl of the genie vase, the old lady sparked a wooden matchstick, lit the substance, and watched intently as the pungent smoke of the fiery black incense wafted through the openings of the genie vase.

"Rocky," the old lady lectured as she moved around the room and circled the silvery genie vase around her body and his, "this smoke will keep away the *Bubak*, the keeper of evil spirits. You are a young child, Rocco, so you must especially be aware of the *Bubak*. If you are a good boy, Rocco, and obey your mother, the *Bubak* will stay away!"

From this indelible memory, Rocky remembered the night he agreed to attend a Smudging ceremony with his shrink. As he learned from his shrink, Smudging is a spiritual ceremony prevalent among Native

Americans. Standing in a dim, lower East Side Manhattan loft, alongside his shrink and part of a circle of five other people, Rocky watched what appeared to be a young Native American woman standing in the middle of the group. Using a large feather and moving slowly around the group, she fanned each person with burning sage smoke wafting from a large clay pot. As she enveloped each person with the smoke, she chanted a Native American prayer in a soft voice. After initially cleansing everyone's soul of evil spirits with the sage smoke, she then took another large clay bowl that contained burning wrapped cedar sticks, which, as his shrink explained, would purify their spirits. Again, she moved around the circle of people and waved the burning cedar smoke using the feather around their bodies. When that part of the ritual ended, the woman took a third bowl filled with burning sweetgrass and performed the same ceremony again. As Rocky's shrink said, this last ritual would impart good influences on him and fill his spirit with good feelings. At first, Rocky thought all this smoky hocus-pocus was colossal bullshit, even though he did believe in good luck charms and talismans. Rocky admitted to himself later, though, that when he returned to New Jersey, he felt like a million bucks. He slept like a baby and never jumped up once during the night from any nightmares. The next day, he shot lights out during a match that netted him close to $1,500. He begrudgingly attributed his good fortune to the Smudging ceremony the night before. It wasn't long before Rocky found himself in a New Age shop on 14th Street near Union Square, buying sage, cedar, and sweetgrass sticks that he could burn at home. Although nobody warned him that Smudging should only be reserved for special occasions, Rocky felt he had only so much good spiritual luck to draw on. He was careful not to overdo his

Smudging rituals between carrying his good luck charms and other little superstitions and traditions he followed.

When he returned home from meeting with Gino at Maximus that evening, and after learning what his life would be like over the next four to eight weeks, and especially fearing his involuntary involvement in Gino's affairs, Rocky knew tonight was a special occasion. In fact, it was an exceptional occasion. He lighted a bundle of sage in a large clay bowl to rid himself of the evening's evil spirits. He hoped that the finishing caresses of the cedar and sweetgrass smoke that he would later dust himself with would soon, God willing, grace him with only positive influences in the days ahead.

10

"Isn't that great news, Rocky?" Howard asked.

They were sitting in the men's grill of Woodland Crest, having a post-round lunch, Howard chewing on his usual burger with cheddar, and Rocky enjoying his chicken salad sandwich.

"Rocky," Howard asked, "you okay? You seemed a little distracted out on the course today, and you're a million miles away from reality here, too. What's up, my man?"

"I'm fine, Howard. Just a couple of things on my mind".

"Anything I can do to help?"

"Nah, tell me more about this Myrtle Beach trip," Rocky said, trying to change the subject.

"It's going to be a great time", Howard said again, fully enthused. "I already canceled The Kids after I heard from a friend named Beau Greene that we were in. A twosome dropped out, and we're taking their place. All I have to do now is call him today to tell him we're confirmed."

"And it's a $300,000 first-place prize?" Rocky said, the potential of a big payday finally sinking in.

"Twosomes are coming in from Florida, North and South Carolina, Georgia, Tennessee, and Alabama," Howard said.

"And it's how much a man to get in?" Rocky asked.

"It's $12,500 a man, $25,000 a twosome," Howard said. "The overall pot is $600,000 because they limit the outing to 24 twosomes. The first prize is $300K, with $150,000 going to second place and $50,000 for third place. The rest of the money goes to renting the course, paying the pros who will run and referee the event, food, hotel rooms, etc. We play a series of round-robin tournaments and then elimination matches in the final round. As I said, it's a three-day tournament during the last week of May."

That last piece of information sent Rocky off to la-la land. The final matches were on Memorial Day, meaning he had to play a round, catch a plane back to Newark that evening, and meet Pete Malone at Fair Play for his first day of "work" the next day. It was all doable, of course, but Rocky was already feeling stressed by all the events that had developed over the last several days. The excellent news, Rocky thought, and indeed a result of the smudging ceremony he had done last night, was that the Vegas trip with The Kids was off. He would have had to cancel Howard on that one. Maybe some positive influences were starting to come back to him after all.

"Okay, Howard," Rocky said, suddenly feeling pumped up. "Sounds good to me. Let's go win some serious money."

"That's the Rocky I know and love!" Howard exclaimed.

The Myrtle Beach tournament format was familiar to Rocky. They were playing a four-ball match play with no handicaps. Most of the guys were scratch or very low, single-digit handicaps. Five nine-hole matches were to be played over the first two days within each group. There were four groups, each group consisting of six twosomes. Each hole won was worth one point, and tied holes were worth ½ point. The winner of each nine-hole match got a bonus point, making the overall game worth 10 points. In the event of a tie for 1st place in a group, a head-to-head match would decide the winning team. On the last day, the final round consisted of the winners of each group playing each other under a single elimination format. In addition to the

Shooting Bogies

$12,500 buy-in money, betting was being waged among the twosomes of each group—$5,000 Nassaus plus a wild assortment of side bets.

When he arrived in Myrtle Beach, the sun was shining, the temps were unusually cool, and the air was still. It was perfect weather for golf. Rocky had played with his share of hustling golf characters before, but never had he played, he thought as he met each twosome, with such a collection of oddballs all converging in one place.

There was the twosome from Alabama, Sauly "The Bunny Hop" Becker, nicknamed The Bunny Hop because, after every swing, Becker performed a little pirouette as he finished each swing. Playing with Sauly was Teddy O'Brien, a smiley-faced teddy bear of a man suffering from chronic flatulence. At almost every hole, while standing over his ball and what had become part of his pre-swing address routine, Teddy would lean left for just a moment to loudly relieve himself of his unending gastric distress. And as Teddy would right himself back to vertical, Sauly would immediately call out and say, "What did you say, Teddy?" At first, Rocky and Howard figured this little act was meant to throw off their concentration. But they later learned that the "Teddy and Sauly Fart Show" was just innocent, infantile behavior that had been going on for more than fifteen years.

Then there was Richie Byrnes, the astrophysicist from Raleigh, North Carolina, who talked non-stop about the physics of golf, from advanced dimple technology on today's golf balls to the "hogwash" of using the plumb bob technique to putt. Richie contended that due to the earth's curvature, employing a plumb-bob was a useless activity that gave you no more a read than if you just looked more carefully at the green. He evangelized his pet theory for three days running, complete with charts he pulled out of his golf bag. And then there was Richie's partner, Vinnie Franco, a flamboyantly dressed dentist from Raleigh. He came to the tee the first day wearing powder blue and white argyle socks, bright white knickers with powder blue stripes down the outside of each leg, and a University of North Carolina powder blue mock turtleneck. In the following rounds, his outfits got even more outrageous. On the second day, Franco was dressed in a black and white knickers outfit, one leg white and the other black. The knickers were matched with a black and white golf shirt in which the all-black side of the shirt was situated above the white pant leg. The all-white side of the shirt was located over the black leg pants. The man looked like a walking piece of pop décor straight out of a Mackenzie-Childs webpage. The coup de grace, though, was the final day when Franco wore a faux camouflage silk outfit. Instead of the typical camo colors of green and brown, Franco's camouflage colors were powder blue and black. He told anyone within earshot that all these outfits were custom-made, sewn by a Dominican seamstress in New York City from his designs. Franco sat on the Board of Trustees at UNC and was a big athletic booster of the college. He had developed and patented a tooth-bonding technology adapted by dentists worldwide. Franco stood just five feet two inches tall, with rosy cheeks. Rocky thought he looked like one of those little Hummel statues his mother kept in her curio cabinet in the living room. He also imagined what the boys back in Belleville would say after taking one look at Franco's outfits.

But the guys Rocky got a kick out of playing with were the twosome from Miami, Mike Quinn and Jules Snyder. Quinn was a highly successful day trader who loved to gamble on the market as much as he loved to bet on his golf game. Quinn had his specially built golf cart shipped to Myrtle Beach for the tournament. The cart was loaded with all types of high- and low-tech amenities. It sported a GPS, a stereo/DVD/Bluetooth player, a mini-refrigerator, an electric club and shoe cleaner, a mini-microwave, a digital library of scorecards matching more than 300 courses in the United States, a built-in club storage rack that rendered obsolete the use of a golf bag, and a mini-Bloomberg stock terminal that kept Quinn informed on his trades and stock holdings.

Snyder owned a successful jewelry wholesale business that serviced major retail chains, department stores, specialty stores, and online sites. Rocky had never seen anyone play golf with the amount of jewelry Snyder wore. The man was a walking jewelry store: His ring fingers were adorned with two-carat diamonds. He wore gold rope chains weighted down with medals. An oversized gold Krugerrand wristwatch adorned his left wrist.

In contrast, his right wrist was ornamented with ID bracelets and gemstone-festooned bangles. When Snyder swung, Rocky thought it sounded like someone shaking three coffee tins all filled with ball bearings. The jaw-dropper, however, was Snyder's cuspids. Snyder had the audacity of implanting small diamond inserts into each cuspid, so when he smiled, especially when facing the sun, he exuded a razzle-dazzle smile. It was the damnedest thing Rocky ever saw, and he wondered how long Snyder would survive walking the streets of Belleville or Newark wearing all his jewelry.

Compared to the colorful cast of characters Rocky and Howard were competing with, the golf course they were playing, Myrtle Beach's Yellow Witch North, was *almost* tame by comparison. The tournament, of course, was being played from the championship tees, which made the course play at slightly over 7,000 yards. Built on a former tobacco farm, it was unique. The front nine played as a links-style course, riddled with links course elements like deep and hidden bunker hazards, unmowed wild grass, wetlands, and gullied greens.

The most notable hole on the front was the 195-yard par-3 7th hole. The oddity of this hole was a pot bunker strategically placed in the heart of the green, effectively splitting the green in half. Every green on the course was lightning fast.

The back nine of Yellow Witch North was more of an American-style track. Many fairways were framed with oaks, pines, and Southern magnolias. Hazards included strategically placed sand traps, marshes, and water. The most challenging par-4 on the back nine was the 426-yard number 14. From the tee was a very narrow fairway between a lake on the left and trees on the right. Almost everyone's tee shot found the lake or the trees during the tournament. The hole played longer than 426 yards because the approach shot was into an elevated green. A front bunker and two very deep bunkers on either side surrounded the green. The pin, positioned in the back right-side quadrant, required putts to be played through a large swale. Moreover, the 14th green was also one of the smallest greens on the course. Scoring par on the 14th was an achievement.

But for Rocky and Howard, pars were scarce throughout the tournament. They would have saved themselves a lot of time and heartache by throwing their $25,000 entry fee out a car window onto Bloomfield Avenue. Individually and as a team, they lost every one of their matches. They got creamed on the overall scores and lost all their side bets, racking their losses to an additional $20,000. Howard's game fell apart altogether. His tee shots never landed on the fairways, his approach shots found all the hazards, and his short game was dreadful.

Shooting Bogies

Rocky, on the other hand, had a more ominous problem. While his tee shots, approaches, pitching, and chipping games were dead on, Rocky couldn't make a putt if his life depended on it. Putting was Rocky's strongest suit, but Rocky routinely missed 3 to 4-foot putts throughout the tournament. Most of these missed putts resulted in him shooting bogies, certainly not even close to a winning score when your opponents routinely are shooting pars and birdies.

There was no question that Rocky's yips stemmed from his nervousness about his new "job" at the Fair Play Country Club. Every time Rocky stepped on a green, his mind wandered off to Gino and what he may have in store for this guy Bogalinsky. Rocky wanted no part of Gino, but he had no choice, given the corner he put himself in. Instead of entirely focusing on the putt at hand, Gino's voice popped into his head just as he was lining up to study his putt. He tried to work through his inner noise, but it was useless. He kept missing putt after putt and racking up bogey after bogey. Rocky found himself enshrouded in a Gino "fog." It was embarrassing for Rocky to have putted so poorly.

Their flight home had just reached cruising altitude as they returned to Newark Airport. It was late Sunday night. Neither Rocky nor Howard had said much to each other about their lousy play during the tournament. They both knew how badly each of them played.

They had gotten their clocks cleaned, and that was that. It was time to go home. Richie, the astrophysicist, and Vinnie, the flamboyant dentist, took home the first-place prize of $300K. A twosome from Georgia took second while the "Teddy and Sauly Fart Show" took third.

But Rocky wasn't making any excuses to Howard, and even if he did, what could he say? Rocky put his head back on his head cushion and thought...

"Hey Howard, there's a reason why I putted like shit. I've gotten myself involved with a mob family. A mob family I've done small but harmless jobs for over the years. They've drafted me to help them in a God-knows-what's-going-to-happen plan against a billionaire named Pincus Bogalinsky. I start working for Bogalinsky tomorrow at The Fair Play Country Club, his golf club. This guy Bogalinsky? He will probably die if he decides to buy Fair Play or doesn't play ball with the Lofaccio clan. That's what the mob does. They see something they like, and they want in.

I start this bogus job tomorrow. Get to know Bogalinsky, Gino says. Chart his activities. Eavesdrop on his conversations. Find out what he's up to. And report back to Gino, the calculating and vicious leader of the Lofaccio clan. From there, Howard, Gino will probably sit down with Bogalinsky. If Bogalinsky tells Gino to screw off, Gino will have one of his men put a bullet in

Bogalinsky's head. Or, one day, Bogalinsky will disappear. Probably both. Either way, I've been involved. See why I putted like shit these past few days, Howard? My whole life suddenly seems like one big bogey right now.

11

Pete Malone was a handsome yet mousy man. The kind of guy alpha males like Gino pushed around for kicks. Malone had deep-set blue eyes, a ruddy upper-Midwest complexion, and Robert Redford blond hair. According to Gino, the big blemish on Malone's resume was his predilections for partying with high school seniors in Motel Six bedrooms. A weakness that Gino was leveraging to full advantage.

When Rocky first arrived at the Fair Play Country Club, Malone greeted Rocky in the pro shop. They looked like The Odd Couple driving around Fair Play in a golf cart. One was a slightly built, fair-skinned farm boy who could double as a Midwest weatherman.

The other was an overweight, balding, dark-skinned New Jersey Italian who was a casting agent's dream for a sitcom pizza man. The two had nothing in common except a debt to Gino Lofaccio.

"So, how long have you been working here?" Rocky asked, trying to make conversation with this skittish guy. They were sitting in Fair Play's empty Men's Grill, waiting for sandwiches they ordered from Maggie, the grill room server.

"Bogie hired me when he took over the place last year," Malone said, nervously drumming his fingers on the table. "Nice place. Easy work. I only have to worry about a couple of foursomes a day. Not your typical golf club. With only 64 members, most of whom are investment banker types, the course sees very little play."

"Who's Bogie?" Rocky asked.

"Pinky is Bogie, Malone said. "Pincus Bogalinsky. He goes by either Pinky or

Shooting Bogies

Bogie, but he prefers Bogie. Plays into his movie star self-image. Didn't you notice the poster in the men's locker room?"

Rocky did. Still, he missed the connection of a framed and autographed Humphrey Bogart *Key Largo* poster hanging in the men's locker with Pincus Bogalinsky. When Rocky first saw it, he thought having a movie poster in the Men's locker room was strange. Plus, it threw off the whole ambiance of Fair Play's sleek, Euro-style decor.

"So, how do I play my role here?" Rocky asked.

"Your biggest responsibility is keeping Bogie and his associate happy," Malone answered, his eyes darting away from Rocky and his finger drumming becoming even more frenetic. Rocky sensed what a pushover this guy must have been for Gino. The guy was afraid of Rocky, too. He acted like he never had to deal with Italians, which he probably didn't. Rocky didn't like that he was making Malone nervous and tried to set him straight.

"Listen, Pete," Rocky began. "I'm here because I owe Gino for something *I did* to his family. It was bullshit, but Gino, the little bastard he is, saw it as an opening and decided to break my balls. I'm in the same boat as you. We got something in common. You try to trust me, and I'll try trusting you. Hopefully, both of us walk away from this safe and sound."

"I don't want to talk about Gino Lofaccio," Malone said, mispronouncing Gino's last name by pronouncing the double c as an s.

"First thing you gotta know, right now, Pete, is that it's Lofaccio," Rocky explained, pronouncing the double c as a soft ch. "Don't mess his name up, Pete. That will piss him off."

"I got myself into a real jam," Malone lamented, his right hand running through and messing up his Robert Redford hair. "I can't believe this is happening." By now, Malone was in full drum mode, fretfully twitching his legs under the table, the leg motions in sync with his drumming fingers. Rocky thought he looked like a cartoon character kicking up dust while running in place.

"You got to take it easy, Pete," Rocky said. "You do what they want you to do and then move on. If anybody besides Gino asks you anything, you don't say anything. You didn't see anything. You didn't hear anything. No matter how nervous you get, try to stay calm. Understand? What's going to happen here, I don't know. The best thing you can do is keep your mouth shut. You do that, and you'll be fine."

"Yeah, I get it, but I don't like it."

"Me neither," Rocky said. "But like I said, just do it and move on. This sure is one hell of a place this guy built for himself," Rocky said, trying to change the subject.

"The previous owner poured nearly $30 million into it," Malone said. "When Bogie came in, he invested another couple of million in sprucing things up. Many of his Wall Street cronies are members. He renamed it Fair Play because the previous owner was a crook who got into tax trouble with the State of New Jersey. The State seized it and is the current owner. Bogie thought the name would be a cute touch since it can have a double meaning."

No question that it was a one-of-a-kind golf facility. Bogie wasn't going anywhere, Rocky thought, especially if he had already invested significant scratch for improvements.

The morning tour was an eye-popper of amenities and décor. A 4,000-foot airstrip and helipad were on the far side of the grounds. A tram and an on-call attendant shuttled members and guests from the airstrip to Fair Play's clubhouse. A wisteria arbor, offering shade, sheltered the path to the airstrip and helipad.

The clubhouse that Rocky and Malone sat in was a homage to understated elegance, exuding a Danish Modernism sophistication. Unlike most clubs, Fair Play's dining and public areas featured a sleek and minimalist design, combining simplicity and functionality. The stark white walls were offset by polished Brazilian walnut flooring and beech tables. Shaded tan and grey hues accented the dining chair and sofa cushions. There was a smart use of natural lighting to give the clubhouse an airy sense. Oversized windows and glass entry doors added splashes of sunlight to its unobtrusive interior. Strategically placed floor, table, and pendant lighting characterized by clean lines offered warm and diffuse light that felt closer to candlelight than harsh lighting. The place was a radical departure from the usual country club clubhouse design.

Because its décor was so unique, Fair Play's dining and public areas had been featured in numerous interior design magazines and websites and received multiple awards.

However, the jewel of the Fair Play Country Club complex was the golf course itself. Rocky recognized this was an extraordinary layout from the first tee box through the 18th green. Not a blade of grass anywhere was out of place. In addition to the meticulous care of the fairways, tee boxes, water and sand hazards, and greens, the course's other surprising features were several modern art sculptures discreetly placed throughout the course. After meeting Howard, Rocky played at some of America's most prestigious golf courses. Fair Play was at the top of the list as one of the best golf courses he had ever seen. For Gino to even consider demolishing this course for another cookie-cutter New Jersey development of townhouses and condos was a crime.

12

"Tell me what you've heard so far."

"Nothing, Gino. I haven't even met Bogalinsky yet."

"Where the fuck is he?"

"I don't know."

"Whaddya mean, you don't know?"

"Nobody's saying where he's at."

"You ask Malone?"

"Sure. Pete has no idea. Bogalinsky comes and goes, which is what Malone says. The only thing Malone is sure of is that Bogalinsky will be arriving with one of his business associates. A woman by the name of Rita Torrone. It's not like he has to tell people what he's up to, Gino."

"Don't get wise on me, Rocky."

"Sorry, Gino, I ain't getting wise. I'm just telling you what it is."

"Find out more. Find out when he's coming to New Jersey."

"I don't know who else to ask other than Pete Malone. He's Bogalinsky's main guy at Fair Play, as you know. Everybody else reports to him. If Pete doesn't know, nobody's gonna know."

"All *I* know, Rocky, is that you haven't found out dick for me."

"I haven't been able to get anything because there's nothing to get."

"You're a shithead, Rocky, you know that?"

This was Rocky's third conversation with Gino during his first week at Fair Play. It was the same thing day in and day out. The conversation just went round and round. Gino was being his usual self, bullying and unreasonable. But Rocky knew better than to push back.

Shooting Bogies

Rocky wanted to ask Gino why he was needed at Fair Play in the first place. Didn't Gino have Pete Malone in place in Fair Play? Couldn't Malone tell Gino when Bogalinsky was coming? Couldn't Rocky make amends to Gino in some other way? Rocky wasn't getting it, but he wanted to avoid challenging Gino.

Rocky knew Gino. When he didn't get the answers he wanted, he became a real pain in the ass. Gino would get pissed just for the show. Or else Gino would go genuinely ballistic, scream and yell for a while, and then cool off. Right now, Rocky had no idea how this conversation would end up.

What Rocky did know was that he had spent the last several days at Fair Play with his pecker in his hand. Outside of unpacking a couple of golf club sets that were delivered by UPS for a few members, playing a daily morning round of golf, and hanging out at the pro shop and grill room with Pete

Malone, nothing else was going on. It was the most boring job he ever had.

The only thing worse was guard duty in Kuwait, where he just sat around and waited for something to happen. Most guys, Rocky thought, would love playing golf every morning. But he was getting more restless by the minute. He missed his rounds with Howard and wanted to return to his routine. Thank God his mother wasn't giving him any headaches. That's all he needed at this point.

"Tell me about Bogalinsky's associate," this query coming from Mrs. Lofaccio, sitting in her usual dark corner.

"I haven't met her yet, Mrs. Lofaccio," Rocky said, wondering if she missed any of his conversation with her son, even though she was sitting not four feet from him. "As I told Gino, Mrs. Lofaccio, Bogalinsky hasn't shown up yet."

"That doesn't mean nothin' to me," Mrs. Lofaccio said. "The bimbo could have still been there."

Shooting Bogies

"Sorry, Mrs. Lofaccio," Rocky said, "I should have mentioned that she's arriving with Bogalinsky." Rocky thought about correcting the old witch by telling her that the female associate was Bogie's marketing consultant, not his girlfriend, and therefore not a bimbo. But he decided to keep his mouth shut.

"Sorry," Rocky repeated.

The three of them were meeting again in Maximus's basement office after Rocky's drive up from Fair Play earlier that night. Rocky felt like he was descending into hell every time he entered this office. He expected to see Gino's inner circle of Vinnie, The Pipe, and Frankie Beep. But Gino and his mother were the only ones there.

"Listen, Rocky," Gino said, his voice rising. "I'm tired of all your fuckin' sorrys. You go find something out. You hear me, you good-for-nothing piece of shit? I've cut you a lot of slack here, Rocky, and you've delivered squat. I gotta know when Bogalinsky gets into town, understand? I need to know when he's going to make his decision."

Rocky already gave Gino his opinion about Bogalinsky's alleged intentions and how Bogalinsky was into Fair Play for millions. But Gino already knew that and said that meant squat. A couple of million to Bogalinsky was nothing, Gino said. It would have no bearing on what Bogalinsky would do. Rocky found this strange but didn't say anything to challenge Gino.

Gino turned his back on Rocky, pushed over a chair, and stormed out of the room.

Rocky was left sitting with Mrs. Lofaccio, staring at him.

"You heard what he said," Mrs. Lofaccio said. "Go find something out. Stop wasting our time. Now get out."

Rocky thought the meeting was pretty tame as he walked up the stairs to leave. On a scale of one to 10, being called a useless

Shooting Bogies

shithead and watching Gino knock over a chair rated a two at best on Gino's ballistic scale.

However, Gino got more belligerent the following week. Several lamps were damaged, two ashtrays were flung, and a broomstick was smashed against Gino's desk—causing the Frank Sinatra bobblehead to really convulse.

And then there was Mrs. Lofaccio cursing and swearing at Rocky in English and Sicilian. The flung ashtrays, broken lamps, and smashed broomstick didn't bother Rocky as much as Mrs. Lofaccio's insults. She was spooking him the most. Listening to the old bag swearing and cursing him and his family, his family's ancestors, and the Delmonico name made Rocky tense. What put an edge on her abuse was that Mrs. Lofaccio was still wearing her mourning outfit. She had been wearing nothing but black since her husband died in May. Watching her sit in a dark corner, hissing away curses and swearing at him in her black mourning garb, was stressing him out. Rocky was so unnerved that after these sessions, he'd drive back to his house and smudge away the evil Lofaccio karma swirling around him. He hoped that Pincus Bogalinsky would show up at Fair Play any day now. He even began praying for Bogalinsky to arrive. Before this last meeting, he had gone to St. Catherine's to light a candle. He said a prayer and promised God that he'd stop eyeballing the cute blond that sat in the third pew at Sunday mass if only Pincus Bogalinsky would appear. Rocky wanted his participation in all this bullshit to end soon. The last ten days were very intense. Meeting every night with Gino was getting crazy. He'd rather stand over a 10-foot putt with 10k on the line than put up with this.

13

"So, you're Delmonico."

"Yes, sir. I'm Delmonico," Rocky said. "Glad to meet you, sir."

"Let's get something straight right off the bat," Bogalinsky said, changing his tone. "Everybody that works for me calls me Bogie. Not interested in you blowing smoke up my ass by calling me sir. Bogie is what I expect you to call me, understand?"

"Got it."

"Good. So, how do you like the place so far?" Bogalinsky asked.

"It's' a great club," Rocky answered. "Magnificent course and a one-of-a-kind clubhouse."

Word spread the day before that Bogalinsky was arriving at the club. Rocky was relieved. He could report something back to Gino. The Fair Play staff was in a frenzy, gussying up the place for Bogie. Pete Malone spent the previous 24 hours meeting with all the club's department managers. He was constantly on his walkie-talkie, staying in close touch with the groundskeeper superintendent, Ben McDonald, asking McDonald for updates and demanding that each blade of grass on the golf course be in tip-top shape. He met several times with the facilities manager, Jack McConnell. He agonized over the next week's menu with Nick DiMartine, Fair Play's chef. And he coordinated last-minute grounds details with Marie-Christine Lamay, Fair Play's full-time facilities gardener.

Until midnight before Bogalinsky's arrival, an army of groundskeepers meticulously trimmed, cut, and rolled every green, fairway, and rough. Work crews were

Shooting Bogies

carefully grooming water and bunker hazards. And Madame Lamay and her staff of gardeners were busy tending to the flower beds and shrubs.

Malone told Rocky that Bogalinsky was arriving by plane. He was flying into the club's airstrip on his Gulfstream jet. And because he had been away for an extended period, he was sure to do a fly-over to check the course's overall condition. If he saw anything he didn't like, heads would roll. Malone described Bogalinsky as a huge man who stood six feet, five inches tall and weighed 240 lbs. But more imposing was his temper. Just last fall, Bogalinsky fired the grounds superintendent because a fungal infestation destroyed a bed of prized rhododendrons that Bogalinsky had imported from Nepal. It didn't matter that Mother Nature was the culprit. Someone had to pay, and it turned out to be the groundskeeper. Never mind that his wife was lying in a hospital, suffering from complications from a difficult pregnancy. Bogalinsky sent him packing not five minutes after he got off his jet.

What struck Rocky most, though, was the pageantry for the big man's arrival. After the fly-over inspection, Bogalinsky, who was piloting the jet, radioed Malone that he was ready to land. This was Malone's cue to ready the staff. As the jet made its final approach, everyone who worked at Fair Play, from the grounds and pro shop staff to the kitchen and the locker personnel, all lined up along the pathway near the clubhouse to wish a hearty "Welcome Back" to Pincus Bogalinsky.

It was a similar welcome Rocky participated in when his army company in Kuwait was ordered to stand at attention as they waited for a four-star General to arrive. But Bogalinsky came in a custom-designed four-seat golf cart resembling a Ferrari Testarossa instead of making a grand entrance in an Army-issued camo jeep. Painted a bright red and sporting the Ferrari signature symbol of a black, prancing stallion on a yellow shield, the cart featured a custom saddle brown interior and a specially designed exhaust system that gave the cart a low, throaty sound. Rocky knew Mike Quinn, the golfer with the maxed-out techno-golf cart he played against in Myrtle Beach, would love this custom machine.

After a few forced pleasantries to everyone on the staff—fortunately, the course's condition was to his liking—Bogalinsky grabbed Malone and Rocky by the arm and led them into the grill room of the clubhouse. Malone then spent the next two hours updating Bogalinsky on the club's business affairs, after which Bogalinsky dismissed Malone with a bejeweled hand wave. Thinking he was also dismissed, Rocky got up to leave, only to hear Bogalinsky order him to stay seated. Rocky sat there for an eternity as Bogalinsky fielded several phone calls on his cell. After a profane scolding to his attorney and one or two other business calls, none of which related to Fair Play, Bogalinsky finally hung up and hitched up his chair to draw closer to Rocky.

"Tell me, Delmonico," Bogalinsky continued, "where you from?"

"From Belleville," Rocky said. "About 25 miles north of here."

"Sure, Belleville. Know the area well," Bogalinsky said. "Lots of Italians up there, isn't that so?"

"That's right, Bogey," Rocky said.

"I like Italians," Bogalinsky said. "Hardworking people. Done well for themselves over the years. But many of them could use more education overall, don't you think?"

"Yes, sir," Rocky said, counting himself as one of those Italians missing a college education.

"And the whole Mafia thing gives your people a bad name," Bogalinsky said.

Shooting Bogies

"Although you have to respect how those bastards go about their business."

Rocky sat back for a moment and thought about that last comment. It was quickly apparent that Gino Lofaccio and Pincus Bogalinsky were cut from the same cloth.

They both were arrogant, had an enormous ego, and needed to intimidate. The only thing Gino didn't share with Bogalinsky was Bogie's penchant for flashing his wealth. It was common knowledge on the streets of Belleville that Gino and his mother were millionaires many times over. But they lived a lower middle-class lifestyle because much of their money was generated through illegal enterprises. But Rocky sensed that even if they had made their money legitimately, Gino and his mother would still live that way. For many Italians, especially the older generation, it was imprudent to show your wealth. Showing off your money would attract all kinds of problems, hassles from the government, resentment from family members, and almost certainly "the evil eye" from jealous friends. It was better to keep people in the dark and have them guessing your net worth than to flaunt your wealth. That was quite a different lifestyle philosophy than most people, Rocky thought, including a guy like Bogalinsky.

"I've had to deal with those Mafia boys at various times," Bogalinsky said, interrupting Rocky's thoughts and not mentioning the Lofaccios by name. "Some of those boys are plain dumb hoods. But a couple are very sharp, too."

"Here's the deal. Tonight Rita Torrone my marketing consultant is flying in. What do you know about Rita?" Bogalinsky asked.

"I don't know too much about her," Rocky answered.

"Goddamm Malone!" Bogalinsky shouted to no one in particular. "He should have gotten you up to speed on *everything*.

Shooting Bogies

I met Rita at an investor conference last November. She's doing marketing consulting for my company. Worked in Europe and South America for many years. Like me, she is the classic overachiever. She got her MBA from Wharton after graduating summa cum laude from The University of Florida. At Florida, she was the women's golf team captain of one of the country's top-ranked programs. A brilliant woman and a real beauty to boot. I'm sure you'll like her."

"She sounds fascinating," Rocky said.

"Oh, Rita is a real pro," Bogalinsky went on. "You'll fall in love with her the minute you meet her. Anyway, she's flying in tonight. Being an avid golfer, she's looking forward to playing Fair Play. Be prepared to play with us. I have some morning teleconferences, so let's plan on teeing off around 2 p.m. Anything else we need to discuss?"

"No, that covers everything," Rocky answered.

"Good," Bogalinsky said as he stood up to leave. "Two p.m. sharp tomorrow. Don't be late. I don't tolerate people who are late. I've fired people who came to a meeting two minutes late, understand?"

"Got it," Rocky said.

14

Playing golf under a hot, mid-June afternoon sun was not fun for Rocky. He much preferred an early morning round, given his low tolerance for heat. But when your boss says to be ready to play golf at two p.m., you hop to it, much like any other working stiff.

Rocky was waiting outside Fair Play's pro shop when Bogie and Rita pulled up in Bogie's Ferrari-styled golf cart precisely at two p.m. Bogalinsky jumped out of the golf cart without acknowledging Rocky's presence and entered the pro shop.

"You must be Rocky," Rita said as she extended her hand, casually dismissing Bogie's rudeness of not introducing Rocky to Rita. "I'm Rita Torrone. It's a pleasure to meet you."

For a moment—though it felt like an eternity—Rocky was tongue-tied. Rita's natural beauty took his breath away. She was the most beautiful woman he had ever met. Her rich red hair glistened under the afternoon sun. She was blessed with heart-pounding, piercing green eyes, and her perfect teeth composed a wondrous smile that never left her face. Rocky felt intimidated and embarrassed just to be shaking her hand.

"A pleasure to meet you too," Rocky replied. "I'm looking forward to our round."

"Me too," Rita said. "Bogie says the course is in great shape."

"Yup," Rocky answered, "the grounds crews…"

"Are we all set to go?" Bogie's voice rudely interrupted. "According to Pete Malone, we have the course to ourselves for the afternoon. "So let's get a move on."

Shooting Bogies

Bogie decided that Rita and Rocky would ride together because he had business calls to make while playing the round. In fact, during the round, Bogie would often tell Rocky and Rita to keep playing through a hole while Bogie pulled off a fairway to make or take a phone call. Bogie dropped off entirely after the 13th hole, leaving Rocky and Rita to play by themselves. Rocky was thrilled when that happened. Waiting on Bogie at the next tee was becoming a nuisance. But more than that, Rocky enjoyed playing with Rita, a woman with a better golf game than most men at Woodland Crest and Fair Play.

It was a blast playing with her. He had never played a round with a woman who scored so well, and he understood how she was chosen to lead the women's golf team at the University of Florida, one of the best collegiate golf programs in the country. The joy of playing and getting to know Rita lifted his spirits over the dark specter of Gino Lofaccio. He was playing like the old Rocky.

Rita told Rocky she was born in Sao Paulo, Brazil, to an Irish-American nurse expatriate named Maureen Casey. Maureen was a free spirit who liked traveling the world after graduating from nursing school. She worked as an ER nurse in six different countries before taking a job at the Hospital Israelita Albert Einstein, one of the best hospitals in Sao Paulo. At Einstein, Maureen met Dr. Marcelo Torrone, a physician who specialized in ER medicine. After a year-long courtship, Maureen and Marcelo got married, and soon after, Rita was born.

"For the first 12 years of my life, I lived in Sao Paulo," Rita said. "I loved living there. It's where I learned to play golf. My parents were passionate golfers who taught me the game and took me along every time they played a round. I was six years old when I first started to play. When

Shooting Bogies

I turned 13, my father accepted a position with a hospital in Miami, so we moved to the United States."

"That must have been difficult for you," Rocky said. "Leaving all your friends behind."

"Not really. My best friends were my mother and father," Rita explained. "We were together, and that was all that mattered. Plus, I immediately began making new friends through golf."

"Where were you playing?" Rocky asked.

"We lived in Coral Gables, joined the Coral Gables Country Club, and played that course. Because I was such a promising junior player—winning many junior tournaments—the Caddie Master at the club asked me to be the first female caddie there. Soon, I became one of the most sought-after caddies at the club. I was carrying bags and reading the greens for some of the top players at the club and making more money than most of the boys."

"That certainly was something you must have teased the boys about," Rocky said.

"Never did," replied Rita. "My parents are very humble people despite their accomplishments. They taught me always to have humility and feel blessed about my achievements."

They drove up to the 18th green, where Bogie was waiting with his Chiclet-tooth 500-watt smile. The sun was setting, and there was a warm glow of light jutting through the trees. Time had flown by. Rocky wished he could go another 9 or 18 holes riding and talking with Rita. He was utterly charmed by the woman.

And it wasn't because of her great looks. She had charisma and intelligence. He looked forward to seeing her again, hopefully soon.

When they arrived back at the clubhouse, Bogie waved him off with a dismissive "good job" and an "I'll see you tomorrow" demeanor. But Rita smiled her wondrous

Shooting Bogies

smile and took her time to thank him for showing him the layout of Fair Play.

"Thank you for playing a round of golf with me. It was great fun", Rita said as she extended her hand for a handshake.

"You're welcome, Rita," Rocky said, his heart pounding. "I'm looking forward to playing with you again, too. Let me add up your scores to tell you what you shot."

"Don't bother, Rocky. I know what I shot," Rita said. "I keep a running tally in my head."

Rocky had played with several golfers who had the talent to keep a running score in their heads. Usually, if they could keep a tally of their scores, they knew what you shot, too. Rocky didn't have that capacity.

"By the way," Rita said, "Bogie is having a little get-together tonight at the house. Why don't you come?"

"Sure," Rocky blurted out, stunned by the invitation that seemingly came out of the blue. "What time?"

"Any time after eight," she said. "See you then."

Rocky was dazed with delight as he returned to the men's locker room at Fair Play. He couldn't believe that Rita had invited him to a party. As he tallied up his and Rita's scores, he discovered she had beaten him by one stroke. Son of a gun. She had to know, Rocky thought. But she was too gracious to say anything. Even so, the day continued to get better, knowing he would see her later that evening.

15

Unbelievable.

That's the only word Rocky could think of to describe his night at Bogie's house. From the moment Rocky walked through the front door, he was dazzled. First by Rita's beauty, attired in a gorgeous summer dress and radiating her ever-present smile as she greeted him. Then she declared Rocky her "party escort" because Bogie kept stepping away to take phone calls in his home office.

Rocky learned quite a bit about Bogalinsky at the party. He was a high-tech whiz, a former electrical engineer who became a highly successful real estate developer. One of Bogie's hobbies was automating everything that could be automated in a house.

Bogie gave Rocky and a few other guests an impromptu tour of his place. It included walk-through demonstrations of the house's electronic capabilities. Every facet of the house was automated: Its security, lighting, heat, air conditioning, music, TVs, computers, home theaters, wireless internet, satellite radio, communications, garage doors, window shading, auxiliary electrical generator, and outdoor spa. A central server operated all these components in an anteroom beside Bogie's office. Bogie archived more than 100,000 songs on the music system alone.

"A buddy of mine in Connecticut has a similar set-up," Bogie mentioned as he walked his guests through the house. "We compete with each other by adding new controls."

"You couldn't have done this all by yourself," a guest asked.

"Nope, don't have that kind of time," Bogie answered. "I did the design but hired a team of electronic and networking experts who did the voice controls, touch pads, security lasers, and sensor installations."

Bogie was eager to show the group the dozens of security sensors and cameras strategically placed inside and outside the house. Every door, window, and pathway had a security sensor. Security sensors alerted Bogie's armed security guard if an unauthorized car came near the house's front gate. The place was secured like Fort Knox.

Rocky was thinking about Bogie's tour as he drove home to Belleville that evening. But more enchanting, he was thinking of his day with Rita. Time had flown by during their round and then at the party tonight. She was so friendly to him that he thought she was playing him for something. But he quickly threw that cynical notion out of his mind. She was for real, and man, what he would do to have a woman like Rita permanently on his arm. But he also knew she was way out of his league. There are lots of reasons to account for that mismatch. But he was thankful for the time he had with her today.

The drive up the Garden State Parkway to Belleville took an hour and a half. Gino had rented a small, furnished apartment near Fair Play for Rocky to stay in. But between the update meetings with Gino and his desire to sleep in his bed, Rocky made the drive home almost every night. When he got onto the parkway, he saw that Gino and Howard had called his cell. He decided he'd wait till he got home to call them back. Even though it was well past midnight, he knew they would both be up—Howard probably in his den and Gino at the club.

Saving the best for last, he called Gino first.

"Just back home after visiting Bogie at his house," Rocky said. "Man, Gino, the guy has some crib. It's set up with all kinds of

Shooting Bogies

electronic gizmos. Did you know he's a former electrical engineer?"

"How about his intentions with Fair Play?" Gino demanded, ignoring Rocky altogether.

"Not a thing," Rocky reported. "Every time he got a call, he went into his office and closed his door. The guy is secretive when talking business."

"Maybe I can get Tony Circuits into his house to bug the place," Gino said.

"That's a huge negative, Gino," Rocky uttered. "The guy's security system is beyond state-of-the-art. I don't think Tony could get within 100 feet of the place. Security sensors and cameras are all over the house, inside and out."

"Thanks for that, Rocky," Gino said. Gino's voice was tinged with satisfaction. "It's about time you got me something I could use." Gino hung up before Rocky could say anything.

Oh shit, Rocky thought. What had he just done? He just told Gino that Bogie's house was heavily secured. He had gotten himself more involved in Gino's business. If anything happened to Bogie, could he be a co-conspirator? Why hadn't he thought about this before opening his big mouth?

To take his mind off what he had just done, he decided to call Howard.

"Hey man, where have you been?" Howard said.

It had been over a month since Rocky had last seen Howard, and it seemed almost a lifetime since they played together at the Myrtle Beach tournament.

Rocky headed down to Fair Play the day after they landed in Newark. As they drove home from the airport that evening, Rocky planned to mention his temporary "golf pro" gig with a bullshit explanation that he was filling in for a friend. But Rocky knew that Howard, the street kid he was, would find all kinds of holes in that story. Luckily, Howard gave him a reprieve when he mentioned he would be leaving in a few days for Hong Kong, staying for about a week or two. Although Howard was officially retired from Crenshaw, he kept himself connected in the global financial game by consulting with several Asia-based companies.

"I've gotten myself a job, Howard," Rocky said. "How about we catch up over a few beers tomorrow night at Woodland Crest?"

Though Howard hadn't immediately responded, Rocky could sense his surprise by Howard's silence. Rocky and Howard had developed a specific conversation tempo, and silences generally were not part of their speaking rhythm.

"Can't do tomorrow tonight," Howard said after the pause. "How you fixed for Tuesday night?"

"Tuesday night works fine, too," Rocky answered. "See you over there about eight?"

"Eight sounds good."

"Okay, see you then," Rocky said.

16

From his seat at the dining room bar at Woodland Crest, Rocky recognized the usual contingent of country club dinner regulars, mainly composed of demanding, grouchy seniors who seemingly lived at the club 24/7. The dining room was also abuzz with the usual assortment of misbehaving, tennis-sweatered adolescents and glum, parent-loathing teenagers. The young brats were being doted on by their blowhard daddies and their over-processed blond mommies. Rocky had nothing in common with these people. The irony was that Rocky drew a crowd whenever he appeared at the club. He knew this was because he was the club's best golfer.

As he quickly learned about country club culture, you can be an axe-murdering lunatic, a high-strung sociopath, a nasty, fall-down drunk, or a moron who couldn't spell his name on a bet. But none of that mattered if you consistently dropped putts from 20 feet out, drove a golf ball more than 300 yards, and posted low 70s scores. You became popular, especially if you showed a little love back to your fellow members.

But the more pressing golf matter to Rocky was the terrible case of the yips he recently developed. The yips, the sudden onset of consistently missing putts, no matter how close you were to the hole, was something that Rocky never struggled with. He had seen the yips numerous times with amateurs of all stripes, especially when there was money, any amount of money, on the table. Rocky saw guys with the yips sweat, shake, and excruciate over a three-foot putt. It's not the money being played for that brought on

Shooting Bogies

the yips. Instead, it's the embarrassment of missing an easy putt. Once the yips get in your head, they stay there getting free rent. They're hard to shake. Every golfer knows that to be a winner in golf, you must be a good putter. The simple fact is that if you're a terrible putter, there is this intimation that you're a choker. And no one, especially the ego-driven country clubber, wants to be labeled a choker.

Rocky was a great putter because he practiced his stroke for hours. The contraption his Uncle Tony built was the perfect putting aid. It consisted of an eight-foot, sawed-off section of a drain gutter, one of those vertical drains that hang from a house roof. The section was glued to a piece of plywood to give it support. Uncle Tony then placed a small wooden shim so that the lip of the drain was flush with the shim. The challenge was putting a golf ball through the gutter drain without letting the ball *ever* hit either side. Rocky swiped the metronome from Renata's piano to develop a putting rhythm—his mother would have killed him had she noticed that he had taken it. He would first set the tempo of the metronome at a certain speed. He would then practice putting the ball with just the right amount of stroke so that it dropped out of the drain's other side just at the exact moment when the metronome ended a certain number of metronome clicks. The speed depended on the length of the imagined putt he wanted to stroke. However convoluted this drill might have seemed to an outsider, it perfected Rocky's putting down to an art and a science. He would practice with this homemade contraption for hours a day, seven days a week. He stroked and stroked, burning in his mind and muscle memory the mechanics of hitting the straightest putts with just the right speed. But his concentration was shot now that Gino had crawled into his consciousness. Whenever Rocky stood over a

Shooting Bogies

putt, Gino's scheme would pop into his mind, and his putting stroke would go to mush. Often, this resulted in very embarrassing misses. It was excruciating at Myrtle Beach with three- to four-foot-long lip-outs. Rocky was alarmed that he missed such easy putts.

Though he had his share of nasty putting streaks, he would always find a quick fix. Rocky knew putting was 70% mental and 30% mechanical. He would spend extra hours practicing his putting stroke in his basement until he was back to masterfully dropping putts. But this time was different. He knew that his putting stroke mechanics were not the cause of the problem. He knew it was because he was a head case. It was Gino that was the problem. Thinking that Gino could do something to Bogie overwhelmed him. He was also upset that he had fed Gino information about Bogie's home security. It was a black cloud hanging out over his head. But what he could he do? Walking away from

Gino was not an option. And just disappearing, like taking the next bus or plane out of town, wasn't a possibility either. Where would he go? Texas? North Carolina? Seattle? Where could he savor Jersey-style scungilli, cannoli, or pasta fagioli in those places?

"Long time, stranger," a voice said, interrupting his thoughts.

Rocky looked up, and Howard was standing next to him.

"Looks like you have the world's weight on your shoulders there, buddy," Howard said. "What's the deal? You haven't been yourself—the weird phone call. Your putting has gone to shit. That's not the Rocky I know. I can tell something's going on. Want to tell me about it?"

Rocky looked at Howard and could see there was no use bullshitting him. Howard was a street kid. It stung hearing Howard say his putting game was in the crapper. But he couldn't disagree. Plus, he valued Howard as

Shooting Bogies

his only true friend. He knew he would be playing with fire by telling Howard about Gino. But he trusted Howard like a brother. He decided right then and there to unload. Hopefully, it might clear his head and help his putting. It could be the quick fix he was looking for. So, just like that, Rocky began telling Howard what he had gotten into by laughing at Gino Lofaccio's mother.

17

On his way home from having drinks with Rocky, Howard had a stress headache that felt like he had been hit by a 2x4 on both sides of his head. Through his years in the shark tank, otherwise known as swimming among predators in the high-finance business world, he was proud he had the skills and intuitive chops to be ready for any encounter. Howard had haggled with the world's sharpest negotiators, savvy business leaders, and hard-nosed lawyers. He didn't get to be the top guy at Crenshaw's Asian office by being timid or getting his clock cleaned on business deals. But as Rocky spilled his guts, Howard sat stunned, caught unaware. He thought Rocky's down-in-the-dumps mood and his bad putting streak were female or golf-related. The last thing Howard expected to hear was Rocky's involvement with the mob and Pincus Bogalinsky.

Rocky asked for his advice three times during their time together, the last time as they said their goodbyes in the club's parking lot.

"What do you think I should do, Howard?" Rocky pleaded. And three times, Howard repeated, "I have no idea, Rocky." And Howard didn't have much to offer as advice. What could he say?

Howard could see the fear and pain on Rocky's face. Howard hoped he wasn't telegraphing his pain and anxiety back to Rocky. What Howard didn't want to tell Rocky, at least not today, if ever, was that Howard was the financing broker behind Bogalinsky's play for purchasing the Fair Play property. It was one of the business deals he worked on during his latest trip to Hong Kong.

When living in Hong Kong, Howard assembled a roster of Asian investors, many of whom he did America-based deals with. He was now coordinating the Fair Play sale through his successor in Hong Kong, Tommy Peters. It was Tommy who connected Howard with Bogalinsky.

Tommy had been at a Crenshaw investor conference at the Four Seasons in Santa Barbara, California when he met Bogalinsky. Bogalinsky was pitching an investor deal regarding a luxury golf course in New Jersey that he wanted to buy. Peters liked the idea and asked Bogalinsky to send him the projected financials of the deal. In the meantime, Peters contacted Hunter Security, Crenshaw's highly trusted corporate investigation subsidiary. It was standard practice at Crenshaw to vet every buyer and seller with whom Crenshaw does business.

Hunter sent over a full report on Bogalinsky culled from a variety of sources. The most compelling finding was that The

Bureau of Alcohol, Tobacco, Firearms, and Explosives had looked into Bogalinsky's involvement with a Syrian-American holding company based in New Jersey, which had alleged connections with the Bashar al-Assad government. But after a year-long effort, the investigation was dropped. It appeared from the sources Hunter Security quoted that the allegations had no merit.

Tommy read the Hunter report and the projected financials and felt Bogalinsky was a reasonable risk, the ATF matter notwithstanding. Tommy then contacted Howard and asked his former boss to be the Crenshaw liaison in New Jersey. Bogalinsky's early life also struck home to Tommy Peters and Howard. He was cut from the same cloth, growing up with nothing and rising to the top—like they did.

The Hunter report read:

Pincus Bogalinsky spent many hours of his youth in the smoky environs of Pappy's poolroom on Chicago's south side. His father, Irving, abandoned the family when Pincus was two. Pincus and his mother rented the apartment above the pool room. His mother was a schoolteacher who had bipolar disorder, so holding down a full-time job was difficult. She worked as a substitute teacher on days when she could. Money was always tight. Pincus got a job downstairs in the pool hall. He worked seven days a week. Watching the register. Running errands for Pappy and some of the pool hustlers. Mopping up at night. Opening the place in the morning before Pappy arrived. Pappy paid the youth a decent wage for his work. And it didn't take young Pincus long to master what you can do with a cue ball. He was soon making extra money hustling pool. Despite growing up in an unhappy and fatherless house, Pincus thrived academically. Inspired by his mother's curiosity and their kitchen discussions on various topics, he was an academic whiz kid.

Shooting Bogies

He also learned street smarts from the pool hustlers, bookies, and small-time grifters haunting the pool hall. When he graduated high school, he was named class valedictorian. His academic achievements earned him a scholarship to The University of Chicago. After consecutive years of scoring a 4.0 grade point average there, he graduated summa cum laude with a degree in electrical engineering. He won a graduate school scholarship to UC's Booth School of Business, one of America's top business schools. When asked what contributed to his phenomenal success, he always cited the great school he attended as a boy— "Pappy's Prep."

Pincus began his career by purchasing distressed homes in the Chicagoland area, fixing them, flipping them, and making a nice profit. He soon amassed enough capital to begin hiring rehab crews on homes he purchased while he searched for more houses to buy. Soon, he moved into building new construction and began amassing a small fortune.

One of Pincus's biggest payouts was a 100-acre plot of land he purchased on speculation just east of the Everglades and several miles west of Miami. One day, he got a call from a real estate broker who told him a Florida developer was interested in purchasing his land.

"Just name your price," the broker said.

Pincus threw out what he thought was a wildly inflated price for the land, but 72 hours later, the broker called back and said he had a deal. Pincus, at the age of 30, was now set for life but was hungry for more deals. He branched out from his real estate development business and invested heavily in high-tech companies. He targeted biotech and robotic companies specifically. His portfolio of companies he owned or invested in spanned 40 different industries. He loved his work, the money he amassed, and his independent and wealthy lifestyle. His only regret, he revealed to a business reporter for a lengthy article on his career, was that he never found anyone to share his life with nor had offspring to continue his legacy.

While his business intellect was honed at UC and Booth, he cited his street smarts and insatiable drive as keystones to his success. He would often boast to anyone who would listen—friends, colleagues, the business media, etc.—that his blended talents compelled him to take *anyone* on in any business deal. And he would further brag that he was usually on the winning side of his deals.

Fair Play wasn't a huge deal, thought Howard after reading the Hunter report and reviewing the financials. Bigger deals usually are easier to finance. But it was indeed a "fun deal" where a few Asian investors could park their money and use the club when they were in the States. From Bogie's end, he would be the managing partner without investing too much of his own money. Howard was excited about the deal and the prospect of playing Fair Play until Rocky dropped his bomb today.

It was clear from his discussion with Rocky that Gino might resort to anything to avoid losing out on Fair Play. But what was Howard to do? The first thing was to get on the phone later that night and call Tommy Peters in Hong Kong to hammer out a game plan for backing out of the deal.

18

Tommy Peters always spoke about his business deals in sports terms. When he was ready to close a deal, he would describe it as being in the "Red Zone" or "in the bottom of the ninth inning."

The day Tommy graduated from St. Barts High School as a star athlete in baseball and a high honors student, he had numerous college scholarship offers. Tommy chose Stanford, a long way from the wood-shingled row house he grew up in Woodside, Queens, but a natural fit for his athletic and academic abilities. Tommy packed his bags, went west, and never looked back.

He was a natural pro baseball pick with his smarts, talent, and size at 6'3" and 210 pounds. Still, he chose his intellect over his athleticism as the fast track to the financially secure promised land. He accepted a full ride to the Stanford Graduate School of Business, graduated first in his class, and immediately joined Crenshaw Securities, a firm that hired smart street guys like himself. At Stanford, Tommy minored in Chinese Studies and became fluent in Mandarin. Tommy knew that Asia was where the future action was business-wise.

The first person he met when he joined the Crenshaw team in Hong Kong was Howard Kinder, another brilliant kid from the streets of New York City. Howard had carved a stellar career at Crenshaw and was the top guy in Hong Kong. It was common knowledge at Crenshaw that Howard was on the fast track to be CEO at Crenshaw. It wasn't a question of if but when. Tommy hoped to ride Howard's coattails. Then 9/11 happened. Howard lost his brother, went off

Shooting Bogies

the rails (as many of his Crenshaw colleagues described it), and quit the firm.

Howard's resignation made Tommy the number one guy in the Crenshaw Hong Kong office. By making lots of deals and posting record revenues, he quickly got noticed by the top dogs in New York. Tommy's goal was to be the CEO at Crenshaw. With Howard out of the way, that was a real possibility.

While Howard stayed with Crenshaw as a Consulting Advisor, his reputation at the firm dropped precipitously. No one at Crenshaw could quite understand how losing a brother (no matter how painful) spurred him to quit Crenshaw just like that. For some members of the Crenshaw corporate team, Howard's resignation was a sign of weakness. It was better, they agreed, the company found out now than later when he was sitting in the top job in New York.

Many brokers in Crenshaw quietly removed Howard from their call list, refusing to have his name on any of their deals. Tommy, on the other hand, maintained a secret affinity for Howard and recognized his business smarts. Still, he kept his overtures to Howard discreet.

Tommy was in the ninth inning on the Bogalinsky purchase, and it was a perfect time to bring in Howard to help finalize the deal. Howard would be Tommy's "man on the ground" in New Jersey.

It was only a $60 million deal, but Tommy deftly negotiated a higher-than-normal broker's fee of 10%. Tommy would have brokered the deal for less. But when he saw Bogalinsky's eagerness to close the deal before the Feds went to auction on the property and how keen the Asian investors were to invest in a jewel golf property based in the United States, Tommy set a priority fee of 10% on the deal.

The sale was set to close in ten days, the papers were sent to New York for final

Shooting Bogies

approval, and everyone was ready to push it over the goal line. But Tommy first had to put up with Howard calling again on his private cell, looking to squash it.

"Howard," Tommy said as he clicked on his cell, "like I said earlier, the deal's done. There's no turning back. Live with it."

"Listen, Tommy," Howard replied, "you and I can live with it, but we're putting a possible bullet into Bogalinsky's head once this deal gets out on the streets. There's no way this deal is going to close anyway. As I explained in my previous call, this mobster Lofaccio will not allow it."

"Not my problem how that plays," Tommy said. "I made the deal, and if it falls short some other way, that's how it goes. New York won't blame me for Bogalinsky getting whacked."

"Is that all you care about?" Howard asked, "Covering your ass? Tommy, where's your sense of humanity here?"

"You're kidding me, right, Howard?" Tommy asked. "This guy's been playing with bad guys all over the world. According to a Hunter Security contact who spoke to me off the record, Bogalinsky is still involved with that Syrian company in Paterson, New Jersey. It has ties with Assad. My guy tells me he doesn't understand why the Feds closed the investigation and walked away. He suspects Bogalinsky might be brokering gun sales between a gun wholesaler in Florida and a pro-Assad Syrian group in New Jersey. So, where's Bogalisnky's sense of humanity here? Helping a tyrant like Assad. If this deal ultimately takes him down, so be it. One less traitorous bastard to deal with."

"So that's it?" Howard asked. "This is your idea of meting out political justice? If you think Bogalinsky is such a bastard, why are you doing business with him?"

"He's been officially cleared by Hunter. I have that to cover my ass. My focus is to

Shooting Bogies

close deals and make money. Pure and simple," Tommy replied. "Whatever comes of the deals is not my problem."

"But Tommy, this close will not see the light of day. As I've said. Lofaccio will see to that."

"What do you want me to do, Howard?" "Tell my Asian guys the deal's off? That is not going to happen. We've spent months putting this deal together, and these guys are jacked to close. I'd lose my credibility here. Maybe Lofaccio is bluffing."

"Lofaccio is not into bluffing," Howard said. "You're a street guy, Tommy. You know how these guys are. Backing down is not in their DNA."

Tommy looked at the clock on his wall. He had another call coming up.

"We're done talking, Howard," Tommy said. "Please don't call again. I won't answer."

Howard was momentarily taken aback by Tommy's rudeness and suddenly realized things would go bad. In addition to the moral consequences of allowing this deal to proceed, he was also concerned about the criminal implications. Would he, Tommy, and Crenshaw be accessories to Bogalinsky's murder?

Howard remembered his earlier meeting with Rocky. There was real fear in Rocky's eyes. An apprehension Howard had never experienced before with another human being. Rocky knew Lofaccio. He had grown up with him and his crew. He recounted some of the crazy Lofaccio war stories to Howard. Lofaccio and the mother were absolute nutcases. And that was based on what stories Rocky knew. God knows what other skeletons Lofaccio had tucked away.

Howard never gave it much thought that he might be one degree of separation from a high-strung New Jersey mobster when he became friends with Rocky. He never met any of Rocky's friends and honestly never wanted to. Howard's time with Rocky was spent in

Shooting Bogies

country clubs, restaurants, local diners, or on a golf course. All of it on neutral ground.

There was that one occasion when he met an acquaintance of Rocky. It took place at the Park View Diner on Route 46. Rocky and Howard sat in a window booth facing the front parking lot. A skinny, somber-looking guy approached the booth, and Howard could see Rocky's face whiten. He quickly recovered and introduced Howard to, as Rocky described it, "a buddy from the neighborhood." Though he introduced him as Louie, he called him Pipe several times. As Howard remembered it, the conversation lasted no more than a minute. It was nothing more than a catch-up chat with lots of "You good?" queries thrown in—and then the guy sauntered off. Howard could sense that Rocky wanted to immediately shift the conversation back to golf, his lousy putting, and an upcoming match. And just like that, Louie, Pipe, whatever his name, became nothing more than a quick, fleeting blip on Howard's radar screen.

Rocky had never been to Howard's house, nor had he been to Rocky's. And all that was fine with Howard. They led separate lives except when golfing or traveling to matches. It was a typical guy friendship, where the bonds of companionship only stretched so far. But now Howard's friendship with Rocky was entangled with Rocky's debt to Gino. And even more ironic was that he was brokering the Bogalinsky deal.

And here he was tonight, arguing with Tommy, a ruthless, young turk he had mentored and taken under his wing. A guy he would have brought to New York with him. Tommy didn't say it, but he probably wished he had never brought Howard into the deal. The last thing Tommy wanted, like any other banker, was news that would threaten a close.

Shooting Bogies

Since Tommy intended to finalize the deal, Howard felt the next step was to tell Rocky what he knew. That he, Howard, was one of the bankers who helped structure the deal.

Howard could convince Rocky to get out of town, improbable as that was for Rocky. Perhaps go to Bogalinsky and reveal what Rocky told him? That would betray Rocky and put both—Rocky and Howard—in the crosshairs of Lofaccio. He could meet discreetly with Jack Berke, Crenshaw's Chairman, tell him what was happening, and hope Jack saw things his way. But in his heart, Howard knew that Jack would side with Tommy. And if he went over Tommy's head, he would forever ice his relationship with Tommy and the other managing partners at Crenshaw. He would be persona non grata at Crenshaw, and the big guys would pull out all the tricks to ensure he didn't latch on with another bank.

As he learned early, scruples had little weight in the investment world. Howard had no viable deal options to play for the first time in a very long time.

19

The irony of the Park View Diner on Route 46 in Clifton, New Jersey, was that there wasn't a park to view for miles. Sandwiched between a Honda dealership on one side and a run-down strip mall on the other, no tree, shrub, or flower bed was to be seen. Park View's frontage, where all the windows were situated, faced Route 46, separated by a pitted, crumbling slab of asphalt pretending to be the diner's parking lot. What little shrubbery the Park View Diner sported had long ago died from benign neglect from Costas Kinelis, the owner of the Park View. Costas, or Gus as his employees and customers called him, was more focused on the eating pleasure of his customers than he was on shrub watering and fertilization. For this reason, despite no curb appeal and lack of dining room vistas, the Park View was a 24/7 dining mecca.

Kinelis was the typical American success story. An early 1970s émigré from Athens, Greece, he landed in Astoria, Queens, to live with his brother, Dimitri. For some unknown reason, Astoria was a hotbed for Greek immigrants to settle into in the early 70s. Some observers speculate that the influx of Greek immigrants was due to Father Papagu, an influential pastor of St. Nicholas Greek Orthodox Church in Astoria. In the mid-1960s, Papagu started a program that welcomed Greek immigrants to the shores of America. He set up job, housing, social events, and small business loan programs to help Greek immigrants assimilate into American society and become successful.

Kinelis got a job as a dishwasher at a diner on Astoria Blvd. He rapidly worked

Shooting Bogies

himself up the organization chart through hard work and a charming personality. And just over ten years after he arrived, Kinelis, with the help of a bank affiliated with Father Papagu's program, became the owner of The Blue Bell Diner, where he had washed his first dish just a decade before. Not soon after that, he met a woman named Irene at a Greek social mixer on the dance floor of the Hotel Roosevelt in Manhattan. It was, as they say in song, love at first sight. Irene was from North Bergen, New Jersey, and the first time Kinelis crossed the New York-New Jersey border, he had flowers (for Irene) and chocolates (for her parents) in hand. One year of romance later, Gus married Irene in St. Athanasios Greek Orthodox Church in Paramus and bought a house there. Soon Kinelis grew tired of the commute from Bergen County to Astoria and sold The Blue Bell at a tremendous profit.

After a year of scouting out New Jersey diners for sale, Kinelis bought the Park View, which was failing miserably under the management of a tired owner. But what the owner lacked in diner operations, he made up for by driving a hard bargain. But Kinelis was eager for the location and was happy to overpay. Kinelis saw the Park View location on Route 46—a highly trafficked New Jersey commuting artery into Manhattan—as a potential gold mine. As he had done with The Blue Bell, Kinelis put together excellent management, cooking, and serving teams. He created an exhaustive multi-page menu whose physical size rivaled The Dead Sea Scrolls. When *New Jersey Inc.* magazine named the Park View "The Best Diner in New Jersey" three years in a row, its popularity soared and became the gastronomic gold mine Kinelis envisioned.

Like any diner worth its salt, the Park View never closed and was open 24/7/365

Shooting Bogies

well before 24/7/365 became an idiomatic fin de siècle buzzword. It catered to all kinds of customers: Harried, take-out-toting commuters; widows meeting for their weekly luncheons; melting pot families of all races, ethnicities, and persuasions; hamburger deluxe-ordering teenagers wandering in on first dates; lonely heart bachelors and bachelorettes—many who ruminatively stirred their coffee and took what seemed like four hours to eat their meals; half-drunk, pre-dawn revelers tunneling or bridging back to New Jersey after partying in Manhattan; and New Jersey wise guys from nearby and far away neighborhoods who huddled together in one of Park View's oversized booths over post-midnight omelets, whispering in hushed tones.

It was because of the sheer number of these wise guys who patronized the Park View that Kinelis reaped new and unimaginable revenue—a stream of "found money" from an inconceivable source—a source that he told no one about, not even his wife, Irene.

He remembers the day when Artie made him the offer. It caught Kinelis completely off-guard. Artie had been coming in at various times over the last several weeks. He was an odd-looking guy with a very long beard who wore a funny hat. Kinelis figured him out for an out-of-towner working at the nearby Nabisco cookie plant down the road. The Park View often was the breakfast, lunch, and dinner haunt for visiting business people working short-term stints in the area.

One morning shift, while pouring Artie a second cup of coffee, Kinelis struck up a conversation. Artie told him he was a visiting chemist doing consulting work for Nabisco. Long ago, Kinelis came to grips with the fact that multi-syllabic-named ingredients that only chemists could pronounce often made up the eye-popping desserts that Kinelis regularly served his customers. Who wanted a

Shooting Bogies

healthy fruit cup when a giant slice of a highly processed, seven-layered fudge cake beckoned from Park View's dessert showcase?

But a week later, Artie came in during lunch and asked to speak with Kinelis in the diner's back office. Kinelis learned that Artie wasn't a visiting chemist after all. After showing him his badge and ID, Artie identified himself as an Alcohol, Tobacco, Firearms and Explosives agent who was in New Jersey on assignment. Artie told Kinelis he and two other ATF agents had been sitting in a van in the Honda Dealership parking lot next door. They were surveilling a couple of wise guys who frequented the Park View. Kinelis, always one who stayed clear of trouble, didn't ask which wise guys, and Artie wasn't saying.

Would Kinelis, Artie asked, allow some ATF techs to plant a series of audio recorders around Park View? For his troubles, Artie continued, he would pay Kinelis $25,000 in cash. Artie mentioned that if Kinelis declined his offer, he would be subpoenaed in light of a pending threat to national security. While all the wise guys Kinelis knew were not guys he'd want to associate with, he didn't think any threatened national security. But what the hell did he know about their business? So Kinelis agreed to Artie's offer, the bugs got planted throughout the Park View one pre-dawn hour a day later, and Artie showed up later that day with a briefcase full of money.

It was near one of these ATF recording bugs that Rocky and Howard sat at a Park View booth after playing a terrible round of golf at Woodcrest. And once they reviewed and agonized over their terrible games, they both knew that the conversation inevitably would turn to Pincus Bogalinsky. The question was who would broach the subject first. Howard decided to take the lead, find out the latest skinny from Rocky's side, and then drop the proverbial bomb: That the deal was done and that Howard was representing the financing firm.

"Let's put golf aside for a moment, Rocky," Howard started, "and talk about your situation. How's it going?"

"Not well," Rocky lamented. "Gino is all over me day and night, asking for the latest news. I don't have squat to tell him. And he's getting more pissed by the minute. I can't keep going on like this. I'm thinking about it all the time. It's ruining my golf. My game has turned to shit."

"No doubt, Howard replied. "Have you seen Bogalinsky?"

"He's been in and out," Rocky answered. "Comes in for a day or two, then flies out on his private jet. I'm playing golf with his business associate, Rita, tomorrow. I'm hoping to learn something more from her. Something that will get Gino off my back. But that's the problem, Howard. On the one hand, if I can get some info that satisfies Gino, he'll finally back off. But then, once he knows the deal is in place, he'll get the ball rolling to whack Bogalinsky. Both ways, I'm screwed, as I'll be the guy who gave Gino the green light. Once Bogie goes missing—which he will, I have no doubt at this point—the cops will drag me in, asking a million questions. Gino will be all over me, making sure I stay quiet as a clam—which, of course, I will. So short-term, long term, Howard, I got trouble now and lots of trouble ahead."

Howard was reeling from what he was hearing. He couldn't believe he was part of a conversation about a potential mob hit. He excused himself to use the bathroom before telling Rocky the Bogalinsky deal was finalized.

Meanwhile, sitting in an ATF recording van in the Honda parking lot just off the Park View parking lot, two agents and Artie were recording Rocky and Howard's every word and getting it all in crystal-clear audio.

Shooting Bogies

"Who the hell is this guy Howard?" one of the agents asked aloud to no one in particular. His higher-ups had ordered Artie to surveil this Rocky Delmonico. It was an unusual assignment—tracking a guy with loose ties to the mob.

"He's Delmoncio's golf partner," Artie replied. "Big-time Wall Street banker. We still don't know how they met, but we're investigating that. Name is Howard Kinder. Had a brother named David Kinder who was on the job in NYC. Lost his life at the Trade Center. Howard is as clean as a whistle, but looks like…"

Before Artie could finish the sentence, Howard returned to the booth, and the agents and Artie leaned back into the audio recording consoles.

"Listen, Rocky," Howard began, "I have something to tell you about the Bogalinsky deal."

Rocky looked puzzled. "How would you know anything about this deal?"

"I'll get to that in a second," Howard said. "What I can tell you is that the deal is done. It closes in 10 days. All the financing and the paperwork have been completed. I tried to stop the deal using my contacts but couldn't. I'm sorry for that."

Rocky was stunned. He couldn't believe that it would be Howard who would be delivering this news. He expected to hear it from Pete Malone, Rita, or Bogalinsky. He regarded Howard Kinder as his refuge from all the crazy shit and people in his Belleville life. He broke that barrier when he told Howard about his Gino situation. But he saw Howard more as a confidante, a neutral outsider. Like his shrink he visited in New York. The last thing he wanted or needed, for that matter, was to have Howard involved in his degenerate affairs. Crying together about losing big-money golf matches and shooting round-losing bogeys was one thing. But learning that Howard knew the Bogalinsky deal was closing soon—before Rocky knew—was entirely different. As a refuge/confidante/outsider, Howard was now a thing of the past.

"How the hell do you know that?" Rocky asked, trying to hide his anger that was swelling up.

"Rocky," Howard stated as calmly as he could. "I am one of the primary bankers financing the deal. I worked with another banker in Hong Kong. A young guy brought me the deal and asked me to coordinate things here in Jersey and New York. That's how I know. After you told me about your problem and involvement, I tried pulling some strings to kill the deal but couldn't get it done."

"You know what you're telling me?" Rocky offered.

"Yes, I do."

"Bogalinsky's dead meat."

"I understand."

"And by you telling me, knowing the consequences, you're involved now, too."

"I understand."

"So what do we do next?"

"You go tell Gino and hope for the best. I don't see any option. Unless you want to skip town and hide like a fugitive for the rest of your life. Or you go to the cops."

"Neither is good. I keep asking, what happens to me next? I feel like I'm caught in a corner and can't figure a way out."

"I know. Me too. I haven't slept in two days. And things will only get worse."

"More for me than you," Rocky shot back.

"True, Rocky," Howard said. "I can't argue with you there. Let's get out of here, Rocky. It's been a long, miserable day."

At that moment, Artie's cell phone buzzed. He noticed it was Janine Cortez, one of his two bosses who was running this case.

"Gotta take this outside," Artie said to the other agents. He stepped out using the van's driver door.

"What's the latest?" Cortez asked abruptly. Typical hard-charging Janine thought Artie. She was cutting right to the chase, not even saying hello.

"We just got Kinder telling Delmonico the Bogalinsky deal has been finalized," Artie reported.

"How the hell did Kinder know that?" asked Cortez.

"Apparently, and coincidentally, he's one of the investment bankers financing the deal," Artie replied.

"Well, this adds a whole new dimension to the case," Cortez said. "Anything else?"

"They talked about Bogalinsky and how he's a soon-to-be-a-dead-man," Artie said.

"And they're both feeling boxed in, scared, helpless, and nowhere to turn."

"Good," Cortez said. "We got them just where we want them." And with that, Cortez clicked off without saying goodbye.

20

What the hell was this? Rocky thought.

What was Gino, Mrs. Lofaccio, Vinnie Bellomo, Bogie, Pete Malone, and Howard doing at this smudging ceremony?

He was in a downtown loft in lower Manhattan. He had no idea how he got there nor who owned the loft. Instead of the empty, sparse loft he was in when he was first introduced to Smudging with his shrink, this space was brightly decorated in blazes of yellow couches, loud abstract red paintings, and bright blue hanging banners and throw rugs. There were odd-looking bird sculptures set throughout the loft. It was eerily dark, with two little halogen lamps casting the only light that pierced through the space.

Gino and Mrs. Lofaccio stood in the smudging circle they all had formed. Mrs. Lofaccio wasn't wearing her smoked glasses. Rocky noticed how odd she looked without her glasses. She and Gino chanted the ritual Native American song that began the smudging ceremony. Next to them stood Bogie, his tanned, lined face framing his high gloss smile. He was dressed in Indian garb, his jewelry a riot of turquoise bracelets clanging around his wrists and necklaces of feathers and gemstones swinging around his neck. He kept throwing his hands up, yelling, "Hallelujah!" He was missing the point of the smudging ceremony, Rocky thought.

Vinnie Bellomo, Pete Malone, and Howard rounded out the circle. Vinnie stood next to Bogie. He was wearing his black suit. His hair was slicked back, and he kept looking around to the others for directions on what he should do. Vinnie looked uncomfortable standing in the circle, watching his bosses singing the Indian

Shooting Bogies

chant. Rocky could tell he wanted out of the place real fast. Just behind Vinnie stood a hunting rifle propped up against one of the bright yellow couches. The cold, dark barrel of the gun stood in stark contrast to the brightly colored couch. It seemed to Rocky that he was the only one who noticed the high-powered rifle. Next to Vinnie was Howard. He was chanting, too. Howard was dressed in an expensive, custom-tailored suit. Rocky had rarely seen Howard dressed up, but Rocky was always impressed when he did.

Standing between Rocky and Howard was Pete Malone. Like Vinnie, his mannerisms implied he couldn't wait for the smudging ceremony to be over, too. Pete kept looking at his watch and whispering to Rocky that he had to leave. "Gotta get back to the wife and kids, Rocky," he said. "Gotta get back now." Despite the urgency of Pete's declarations, though, he never once attempted to leave, nor was anyone in the circle paying attention to what he was saying.

To Rocky, the setting was uncomfortably odd. It was all so out of place. He had difficulty comprehending the incongruity of seeing these people all in one place.

Suddenly, a familiar voice behind Rocky joined in on the chant. The music coming from the speakers above grew louder. It was Rita's soft feminine voice. Gino and Mrs. Lofaccio continued to chant. Bogie yelled, "Hallelujah!" punching the air with his braceleted fists. Pete Malone kept drawing nearer to Rocky and continued to whisper in his ear. The music got louder, its rhythm becoming deeper. Oddly, Vinnie and Howard joined hands and began singing the chant. Although everyone was singing, Rocky sensed they had all drifted to another place. The smudging smoke began to waft around Rocky. He saw it was Rita who was waving the small crucible that held the smoking smudging stick. Rocky noticed a naked body move to his left through the shroud of the smudging smoke. As he looked closer, he saw that it was Rita, totally naked, save for a small Indian

Shooting Bogies

feather pinned in her hair. Her skin was white as snow, and she moved with a ballet dancer's grace. She was moving slowly counterclockwise around the group. She was softly repeating some prayer. Rocky recognized it as a prayer to the Indian gods to remove all negative energy from the room. As she drew closer to Gino and Mrs. Lofaccio, she began smudging them with the sage smoke. Both continued to chant.

As Rocky watched, it appeared that Gino and Mrs. Lofaccio started disappearing. Their bodies got thinner and thinner until they were no more. It was as if Rita was using the sage smoke as an eraser to remove everyone from the room. As the music continued, Rita slowly moved to Bogie and Vinnie. Her naked form was wrapped in sage smoke, and she looked like a beautiful mystical goddess. As the smudging smoke encompassed Bogie and Vinnie, they began to disappear, too. Now, only Howard and Rocky were in the room. He hadn't noticed, but Pete Malone had disappeared. Then Howard faded from view.

Rita stepped closer to Rocky. He was alone with Rita. She drew closer with the smoking sage. Rocky noticed that he was now naked. The smoky crucible that Rita was holding had vanished. She reached out, softly held his face in her hands, and passionately began to kiss Rocky. Their bodies merged, and Rocky could feel her skin's heat and soft gentleness. It was the most blissful and joyous sensation Rocky had ever experienced. They slowly fell to the floor, still fully embracing each other. And in a moment, they were gently making love. But then, just like that, Rita suddenly morphed into a sneering witch, pointy black hat and all, resembling The Wicked Witch of the West from "The Wizard of Oz." She began laughing at him and calling him cruel names.

Rocky woke up with a start, sweating profusely.

21

The drive down the Garden State Parkway between Belleville and Egg Harbor Township, just outside of Atlantic City, where Fair Play was located, was a 125-mile stretch of New Jersey traffic. With the Governor up for re-election, the parkway was usually congested at various intervals with election-year construction zones emblazoned with signs that read "Your Taxes at Work." They were posted next to a photo of the Governor's smiling face. Despite the numerous orange construction barrels and striped barricades detouring motorists, it never seemed anyone was at work. How the tax dollars were at work was anyone's guess. But in New Jersey, a State known for contract kickbacks, cronyism, feather bedding, paid absentee jobs, and the more garden-variety backroom bribe, if you were a New Jersey taxpayer, chances are part of your April tax payment was underwriting some political hack's palatial lifestyle.

Rocky made it a practice to avoid this road congestion by leaving early in the morning or late at night when he commuted between Fair Play and Belleville. During this alone time in his van, he would take stock of the crappy turn his life had taken. Like the New Jersey roads he was driving on, his life had become littered with hazards, bumps, and dangerous curves. He couldn't believe the mess he had gotten into by simply laughing at an inappropriate moment. Instead of being on the golf course working on his game, Rocky was worrying about just staying alive. And to top it all off, the one friend he thought was a comforting refuge from his soon-to-be-criminal predicament yesterday revealed that he too was embroiled, however

Shooting Bogies

unwittingly, in Rocky's mess. The days of talking sports and golf strategies with Howard Kinder—at least for now—were over. Rocky and Howard had bigger fish to fry, like how to stay out of prison on accessory to murder and conspiracy charges. Gino surely didn't like loose ends, and as Rocky figured it, he and Howard were as loose an end as you can get. Despite all this, when he would meet with Gino tonight at his club, he would disclose that Bogie had gotten the financing and the deal was ready to close.

Rocky knew this would set a probable hit on Bogie in motion. He shuddered just thinking about it, but what could he do? Going to the cops wasn't an option.

Ratting out Gino and Mrs. Lofaccio and running was not Rocky's idea of how he wanted his life to go. And not telling Gino was potential suicide, as was giving Bogie the heads up. Because none of these options worked, Rocky saw no choice but to play along and hope for the best. He would rather deal with cops than with Gino. The immediate concern, however, was his 9:00 a.m. round of golf with Rita, a woman he had dreamt he had made love to just the night before. That disturbing memory and the fact that he would set a hit on Bogie in motion troubled Rocky greatly. But he would put on his best face and do his best to act as normal as possible, realizing his new normal had taken on a whole new meaning.

As he pulled into Fair Play's parking lot, Rocky's thoughts oddly turned to Yvonne Mirinovich, a red-headed, green-eyed beauty Rocky fell in love with when he was a 9-year-old at St. Catherine's elementary school. In the 4th grade, Yvonne had all the goods: beauty, book smarts, and musical talents that were best in the school. If St. Catherine's had kept a Hollywood A-list, Yvonne Mirinovich would have placed number one on the list. The most attractive aspect about Yvonne was

Shooting Bogies

how pleasant she was, a classmate who never once said an unkind word to or about anyone.

For all these reasons, many of the boys in her class, including Rocky, were smitten with Yvonne. They would do all sorts of crazy things to gain Yvonne's attention, from bicycling past her house and faking a crash in front of her as she sat on her stoop to secretively placing in her knapsack small pieces of paper that had their telephone numbers on them, with the hope of having her call them. Of course, she never called any of her suitors and just giggled on her stoop when she witnessed yet another fake bicycle crash. But this endeared her even more to her prepubescent admirers. Rocky was part of the Yvonne Mirinovich "Adoration Society" but was its only member whose passion for Yvonne ended up as a disaster. It also foretold Rocky's future relationships with women.

Rocky and his fellow students were in St. Catherine's schoolyard on a chilly November afternoon. They were attending what passed as their phys ed class, which at St. Catherine's consisted of a disorganized mishmash of boys playing tag or engaging in other schoolyard shenanigans and the girls standing around in little groups or simply jumping rope. St. Catherine's was like other Catholic elementary schools: It was great at whipping your soul into tip-top shape but ignored any physical fitness regimen to keep your young body fit.

Rocky was hanging around with a small group of classmates in a remote corner of the schoolyard. He was doing nothing but staring along with other boys at Yvonne across the way. It was communal puppy-dog mooning at its best.

"Hey, Rocky," said Dominick Amonte, one of the boys in Rocky's group. "I'll give you a dollar if you go over to Yvonne and put your arm around her. Bet you don't have the guts."

"No problem doing that," Rocky responded, feeling his young oats. "Show me the dollar."

After Dominick waved a crisp dollar bill under his chin, Rocky walked over to Yvonne and put his arm around her shoulders. The gesture lasted no more than two seconds. Before Yvonne had time to twist away, Rocky was walking back to his group and sporting a big Rocky Delmonico smile as he snatched Dominick's dollar bill. Soon, the school bell rang, prompting the class to line up and walk back into their classroom. Rocky took his place in line and followed his classmates into the school. Suddenly, a voice called, "Mr. Delmonico, step aside and wait by the door."

The voice belonged to Sister Monica Olivia, the schoolyard monitor of the day and the most feared nun at St. Catherine's. Sister Monica was an intimidating presence at well over 6 feet tall, plagued with a scowling face, a man-like, broad-shouldered frame, and a nasty personality. Parish gossip was that St. Catherine's was the sixth school she had worked for in six years. She got along with no one: parish priests, fellow nuns, terrified students, and parent parishioners.

Rocky stood near the door, wondering what Sister Monica wanted with him. After the class had filed in, she finally focused on him.

"Put out your hands, palms up," Sister Monica ordered.

Rocky did as he was told, and suddenly, Sister Monica produced a brass 18-inch ruler from underneath her nun's tunic. Without any explanation, she angrily spanked Rocky's palms with her heavy ruler six times before she stopped. Stunned, Rocky wanted to cry but knew better not to.

"Mr. Delmonico," she hissed, "you should never touch a young lady, especially one beyond your station. You are as low as it gets. Never let me see you touch Yvonne or any other girl again. Do you understand me?"

"Yes, Sister," Rocky said, his palms stinging like crazy.

"Now, return to your classroom," she scowled. "And remember, I'll be watching you."

While the palm spanking hurt through the next day, Rocky's real long-term pain from that encounter was the implication from an authority figure of his being inferior to beautiful girls. As a fourth grader, he didn't wholly understand what Sister Monica Olivia meant when she sneered that Yvonne was "beyond his station"—though he did come to realize its meaning later—but it was like a face slap when she added that Rocky was as "low as it gets." This mean-spirited remark made Rocky's eyes tear up as he turned to return to school—a lack of self-esteem that he carried through life. And he felt he was indeed "as low as it gets" as he walked into

Fair Play to meet Rita for a round of golf. Knowing he would be the instigator in her boss's murder.

Walking into Fair Play's dining room, he thought seeing Rita and the mousy Pete Malone huddled together at a back corner table was strange. The space was empty except for Rita and Pete, and she angrily spoke to Malone. This was not the delightful Rita Rocky knew, but as soon as they saw Rocky approach, Rita and Pete's demeanor instantly changed. Rocky pretended to miss the sharp exchange, wishing to mind his business.

"Hey, Rocky," Pete said. "You're early. I'll get your golf cart ready." And with that, Pete jumped up from his seat and sprinted out of the dining room.

"And Rocky, how are you this fine day?" Rita asked, totally ignoring Pete's odd sprint from the dining room.

"Just fine," Rocky lied. "Just fine."

Shooting Bogies

"You don't look yourself, Rocky. Are you sure everything's okay?"

"All good, Rita. Shall we get going?"

"I'm all set," Rita smiled.

As Rocky and Rita played the course, Rocky noticed a definite distance between them. Rocky was out of sorts with his meeting with Gino looming, but it was more than that. Rita was showing an icy coolness he had not seen before—no easy joking, no smiles, and certainly no warmth. Even more alarming, she was asking lots of questions, probing his background.

She inquired about where he grew up (born and raised in Belleville), how he got into golf living in Belleville (through his Uncle Tony), what he did in the Army (ambulance driver), what he was doing before Fair Play (informally teaching and playing lots of golf at Woodland Crest Golf Club) how he got the job at Fair Play (through a mutual friend of Pete Malone, as Gino told him to say) and what were his ambitions after Fair Play (staying alive, Rocky thought, but said he wasn't sure). Rocky couldn't figure out why she was going on and on with all these questions.

Although he answered all of them to her and his satisfaction, he was so unnerved by her constant queries that he kept missing par putts hole after hole. It was a disaster of a day, and he was happy when the round was over.

Later that day, he was a basket case when he got to Gino's. Does he tell Gino about Rita's curiosity or not? By telling Gino, he will again be an accessory to murder if Gino does something to her. But if he doesn't say anything, and Gino somehow finds out, what would be the consequences to him?

"So, what do you got?" Gino barked as Rocky walked into the room. Gino not giving him time even to sit down, as if Gino already knew the answer.

"The deal's been completed," Rocky reported.

Shooting Bogies

"Who told you?" Gino asked.

Rocky hesitated for a few seconds, dreading bringing Howard into this mess, but he had no choice. Howard understood the possible ramifications but gave Rocky his blessing yesterday to tell Gino he was Rocky's source.

"WHO TOLD YOU!" Gino screamed.

"Howard told me. My friend, Howard Kinder. He got Bogie the financing. But he had no clue you were interested in Fair Play," Rocky quickly added. "He makes these kinds of deals all the time. He doesn't even know Bogalinsky."

"That rat bastard! I'll kill him!" Gino exclaimed.

"Who?" Rocky blurted out without thinking.

"I'll kill them both!" Gino said. "Did you know Kinder was making this deal?"

"Absolutely not," Rocky answered, not mentioning he had told Howard about his involvement with Gino. "I found out when Howard told me the deals he was making in New Jersey."

Gino was pacing around the room like a crazy person, and Rocky could see the wheels spinning in Gino's head, plotting his next move.

"But Gino, I think we got another problem," Rocky said, deciding on the spot to tell Gino about his day with Rita.

"Oh yeah, what's that?" Gino replied, beginning to calm down.

"I played golf with Bogalinsky's associate today, and she asked me lots of questions. She asked me how I got the job at Fair Play, who recommended me, where I worked before Fair Play. All kinds of stuff. She's never talked to me like that. I got a feeling she doesn't trust me or something. Like she knows something's up."

"Don't worry about her," Gino said, waving his hand dismissively. "She'll go away once we take care of Bogalinsky."

Shooting Bogies

Rocky was surprised at Gino's dismissive response, first for not asking him how he handled all of Rita's questions. But also knowing all too well that Rita might be a suspicious loose end if something happened to Bogalinsky. But Rocky wasn't about to stoke Gino's fire any further, so he just stood there waiting.

"You can go, Rocky," Gino said. "You'll hear from The Pipe in a few days."

And with that, Rocky walked out, still not believing he would soon become an accessory to Bogalinsky's murder.

22

ATF Special Agent Arthur Zimmerman sat in a nondescript conference room in Newark, New Jersey, waiting for his colleague Janine Cortez to make her appearance. Janine was known for being late to meetings, so Zimmerman pulled out a crossword puzzle book to bide his time. For Arthur, or Artie, as friends and colleagues called him, solving crossword puzzles was a way to relax and think about his assigned cases.

In front of him sat the transcript of the Howard Kinder/Rocky Delmonico conversation he recorded just several days ago at the Park View Diner. Just to the side of the transcript was a manila folder filled with photos of Kinder and Delmonico, each digitally time-stamped and identified and indexed by an alpha-numeric case number. For the last 20 years, Artie had worked in the ATF intelligence research section, collecting evidence and documentation supporting undercover op agents in gun trafficking, arson, and alcohol and tobacco criminal cases. In each case, Artie precisely knew the goals of the operation. But for some inexplicable reason, this case smelled different.

First, there was Janine, an undercover ops agent with whom Artie had worked for years. Janine was known as a straight-up, seasoned agent who told her colleagues and bosses what was on her mind. She was always focused and mission-driven. But her demeanor, in this case, was off-kilter. Over the last several months working on this investigation, Janine increasingly became edgy and tense—especially the last several days since the Kinder/Delmonico conversation. On the face of it, it appeared Cortez had both Kinder and Delmonico exactly where she wanted them, as she related to Artie when she called him while he was in the van outside the Park View Diner. But since then, her manner had radically changed. And Artie wasn't exactly sure why.

Then there was Paul Reynolds, another undercover agent on this case. He had been tracking Pincus Bogalinsky for more than a year, probing rumors and underworld chatter that Bogalinsky was trafficking firearms to a New Jersey-based organization sympathetic to Assad's government in Syria. Reynolds was using another team of intel gathering led by Saul Rubin. Rubin was a great agent and always collegial. But while working the Bogalinsky case, Rubin had become distant and brusque, never once giving a clue on what evidence was being discovered about Bogalinsky, even though it was obvious to Artie that they were both collecting evidence for the same case. Saul's response was always the same when Artie asked about the case: "Go ask Paul."

And how did Gino Lofaccio, a mid-level, albeit lethal, mafioso based in Belleville, New Jersey, fit in this case? This crazy-ass mobster was out to kill Bogalinsky because of an impending real estate deal Bogalinsky was ready to ink. So why wasn't Janine jumping all over Lofaccio when she learned of his plan? It wasn't like her to ignore a lead such as this one. And why weren't we all meeting as a team? What was with all of the individual meetings and debriefs? It seemed sideways and dysfunctional, with too many whys hanging out there like dangling participles.

Artie contemplated all of this in the quiet of the room. Suddenly, he found it oddly ironic and amusing that just as Janine came rushing into the conference room, Artie finished his crossword puzzle by filling in the six-letter answer for 72-across, which read: *Hot Pavement Optical Effect*. Artie's answer?

Mirage. It summed up the mystery and his feelings about this case like a dream.

After she burst into the room, Janine leaned over the conference table. She slid the transcript and photos closest to her without saying hello. Janine sat and studiously reviewed the transcript and photos. Occasionally, she would look up and ask Artie a question. Artie sat at the table feeling like a mope, wondering whether it would piss Janine off if he re-opened his crossword puzzle book and started a new game. That could get her attention, he thought.

But then, midway through the "meeting," Paul Reynolds came into the room, and she passed over the transcript to Paul and put her focus on the photos. They began talking in clipped sentences as if Artie wasn't sitting there, corroborating an earlier conversation they surely had before coming into the room. Artie was fed up with all this secretive bullshit and decided to speak up.

Shooting Bogies

"So, Janine," Artie started, "what the hell is happening here?"

"How so?" Janine responded, not looking up from analyzing the stack of photos.

"How so?" Artie angrily repeated. "All this secrecy between you and Paul is a prime example. We're supposed to be a team here for Chrissakes. I'm feeling boxed out, not knowing what the hell is going on. We got all these actors: Delmonico. Kinder. Bogalinsky. Lofaccio. All in our crosshairs. We got a possible hit on Bogalinsky coming, but nobody seems to be addressing that. How does it all tie in?"

"You already know John Whitney has termed this case as a need to know," Janine said, finally looking at Artie with a mean-spirited glare. Janine was pissed at Artie for pushing the issue.

Whitney was the Newark Field Division's SAC—Special Agent in Charge. He was the top dog on Newark's field team. He was a tough nut that ran Newark like a military unit. No one ever challenged John. But Artie decided to push Janine a little further anyway.

"Why is the case on a need to know?" Artie demanded.

Janine's face grew flush with anger. Artie could see rage bubbling up inside her. He had never seen Janine so furious, and she wasn't answering Artie's question. Artie looked over to Paul and saw Paul's jaw and cheeks clenching. Artie could tell Paul was itching for a fight. After her rage boiled down, Janine spoke in a very measured, lecturing tone.

"Artie," Janine began, "we've worked on many cases together. And we've all developed a bond of trust with each other. This case is unique and delicate, including how Paul and I work it undercover. It would be best if you trusted John's decision and not ask me, Paul, Saul, and John any more questions about the case. Understood?"

Artie sat, pissed at Saul for ratting him out. But Artie knew he had crossed a line with Janine and Paul, so he decided to stop pushing.

"Understood," Artie responded, simultaneously opening his crossword puzzle book while Janine and Paul returned to their work.

While Artie worked on a new puzzle, Janine and Paul exchanged cryptic comments about the transcript and photos. Although Janine was still simmering about Artie's constant querying, she understood where he was coming from. The long hours invested in collecting evidence through audio or photography are tedious. Not knowing the context of what you're capturing on video or a wiretap of a case can make it even more so. Janine had worked numerous cases with Artie and always found his work top-notch. He was a key figure in all her cases. But not everyone, including the short-tempered Paul sitting next to her, found Artie easy to work with. Paul was a former Marine brought into Newark when John Whitney was named Special Agent in Charge. He was loyal to John and did not tolerate challenges to Whitney's leadership. Artie was not Paul's cup of tea. Artie was a quirky guy who looked like a refugee from a ZZ Top concert, replete with a half-foot-long beard. He had a bushy mop of hair and wore clothing from the 80s, including a Nudu beanie, an homage to Billy Gibbons, ZZ Top's guitarist. Plus, Artie did have, as Janine privately acknowledged, the annoying habit of asking too many questions.

He also irritated Paul with his obsession with crossword puzzles. Artie often pulled out a crossword puzzle when he grew bored attending a meeting. But somehow, he was spot-on with his analysis when he was called on to offer input. John Whitney learned to work with Artie and forgive him for his eccentricities. Because of the dangerous course the Bogalinsky case was taking, Janine felt good about the core team—Paul, Saul, Artie, and herself. She knew they were the A-team in Newark despite the personality conflicts.

"I've read enough," Paul suddenly said. "I'll see you later, Janine." Ignoring Artie, who was deeply entranced with his crossword puzzle.

"Okay," Janine responded. "Let's touch base later in the day."

After reading the Delmonico/Kinder transcript and seeing photos of Delmonico leaving the Lofaccio house, and a transcription of audio recorded from Lofaccio's office at his club—Artie performed a miracle to make that happen—Janine knew she had enough evidence on Delmonico and Kinder for conspiracy to murder Bogalinsky. She knew her leverage over both was enormous and planned to use it to the hilt.

At the same time, she felt sympathy for them. Both were decent men who got caught up in a complex case. They were essentially collateral damage. And you couldn't have two more disparate individuals. One was a ne'er-do-well Jersey guy, a 34-year-old who never got out of his neighborhood despite a tour in the Gulf War. And the other was an international financier well-known as a genius dealmaker in the investment industry. A guy who, until the horror of 9/11, was poised to run one of the top investment companies in the country.

Somehow, they became friends through their love of golf. And fate, through Rocky's acquaintance with Gino Lofaccio and Kinder's role financing Pincus Bogalinsky, brought them into the crosshairs of the ATF. Of the two, Janine felt bad for Rocky, the guy with the more fragile personality. Kinder, Janine knew, was a guy used to swimming with sharks. But Delmonico was in over his head here. She sensed his conflict and pain as she read through the transcript and studied his

Shooting Bogies

I-have-the-whole-world-on-my-shoulders comportment in the photos before her.

Yesterday, she saw it live and in person. It was excruciating watching him squirm. Although he tried to hide it, Rocky was fidgety, tense, and ill at ease when she questioned him during their round of golf while Janine worked undercover as Rita Torrone, Pincus Bogalinsky's business consultant.

23

While Janine pored over Artie's audio transcripts and photos, her thoughts drifted off to her life as an undercover agent. The occupational fear of inadvertently betraying her alias, being discovered, and facing possible lethal consequences was part of every undercover operation. The good news was posing as Rita Torrone replicated a few of her own real-life experiences, making playing Rita easier when compared to roles she adapted in past ATF operations.

Like her undercover alias, Rita Torrone, Janine Cortez was the only child of two high-achieving parents. And like Rita, Janine had an MBA in marketing. While Rita was portrayed as a competitive collegiate golfer from Coral Gables, Florida, Janine honed her scratch-handicap golf skills on Long Island and Connecticut country club courses as a country club kid. But the similarities ended there.

Janine was awarded her MBA from Columbia University, not The Wharton School of the University of Pennsylvania. As an undergraduate, she attended The John Jay College of Criminal Justice amidst the concrete jungle of Manhattan's West Side and not the leafy campus of The University of Florida that was part of Rita's bio. When Janine graduated from Columbia and began her field training with the Alcohol Tobacco Firearms and Explosives agency, her alias Rita was consulting to Fortune 500 companies in South America and Europe. If anyone checked her background, Rita Torrone existed too, but only on paper. The ATF made sure of that.

Janine's high-achieving parents disapproved of her decision to join the ATF after Columbia. Her father owned a successful cybersecurity company that was on retainer with many Fortune 500 companies. He was an internationally acclaimed expert and lecturer invited to speak at worldwide conferences. With an MBA in Marketing from Columbia and a Bachelor of Science in Fraud Examination and Financial Forensics, Janine was the perfect candidate to expand her father's security business. On the other hand, Janine's mother was a founding partner and CEO of MacDonald Neal, a successful investment banking firm specializing in mergers and acquisitions in the media business. Like her husband, she was a recognized leading expert in her field. She was hoping Janine would come to work for her as a senior due diligence specialist. But Janine did not consider either her father's or mother's entreaties. Instead, Janine's career aspirations

Shooting Bogies

were inspired early in her life by her mother's brother, John.

John MacDonald was a New York Police Department officer who worked undercover. He was a highly decorated policeman who worked throughout New York City. At various times, "Mac" worked disguised as a rabbi, priest, cab driver, street cart hot dog vendor, indigent person, construction worker—just about any character in the New York City landscape. The most unforgettable memory Janine remembers of her Uncle John was when he arrived for Christmas Eve dinner when Janine was ten years old. He showed up dressed as Santa Claus and told Janine how he was a police officer masquerading as Santa Claus to catch bad guys.

Throughout her life, Janine thought her Uncle John was the coolest and most free-spirited person in the family. Not chained to a desk like her parents. And she loved his stories about real-life illusion and deception.

His work was her motivation to choose John Jay College of Criminal Justice over more prestigious schools that were beckoning. And when Janine embarked on her two-year MBA work at Columbia, she knew it was nothing more than a parents-satisfying detour before starting her career with the ATF.

Several weeks before she was to fly to Washington, D.C., to begin her training with the ATF, she met with her Uncle John at his favorite watering hole on the Lower East Side to discuss her intention for undercover work and to say their goodbyes.

"I'm not here to discourage you about your plans with the ATF, Janine," her Uncle John began. "But there are things about undercover work that Hollywood never portrays, and more importantly, nobody ever talks about."

"Go on," Janine beckoned as she folded her arms and sat back on her side of the booth.

Shooting Bogies

"Undercover work takes a toll. The fear of discovery will be your biggest demon when you're working undercover," Mac continued. "You'll have stress and bouts of anxiety morning and night. You have to learn how to live with fear, which doesn't lessen with more experience. Every operation has its bad guys who will think nothing of killing you in a New York City second."

"I get the risks, Uncle John," Janine answered. "It comes with the job."

"Knowing the risks and dealing with constant fear is totally different," Mac explained. "Knowing the risks will not diminish your fear of physical harm or violent retribution that could end your life."

"Are you trying to talk me out of not taking this job?" Janine said teasingly. "Did Mom put you up to this?"

"You know me better than that," Mac answered. "All I'm doing is giving you real-life insights into the job. There will be times when you will feel isolated. And lonely. No matter how big your backup team is. You'll become overly suspicious of people. And your personal relationships will suffer."

"Is that why you never married"? Janine asked. She immediately regretted asking her favorite uncle such a personal question, even though she wondered why such a handsome man never married.

"Janine, my personal life suffered because of my job. No question about it," Mac revealed. "But there is nothing I would change. The challenges of undercover work are like no other enforcement job. You must be detail-oriented. Have a strong memory. Stay focused on your target or targets for long periods of time. Have the unique ability to assume different personalities and play every role convincingly."

"Right now," Janine stated, "my career in enforcement is more important than any intimate personal relationship. I'm looking forward to getting it going."

"Well, you're starting with the right mindset," Mac said. "But your perspective will change in later years. Keep this in mind. Undercover is not a James Bond movie. He'd last five minutes in real life. There's no glamour in this job. The boundaries of your life will change constantly. You may even find sympathy for or come to like the targets you're investigating. But you have to disclaim any good qualities they have."

"Despite all the pitfalls, Uncle John, you've been undercover for many years," Janine said.

"Longer than most, Janine," Mac said. "The best undercover enforcement officers guard against burnout. They develop a variety of coping mechanisms. They work with a shrink before, during, or after an operation."

"So you've worked with a shrink?" Janine asked.

"To keep me centered and sane, yes, I have Janine," Mac answered. "Working undercover is an up close and personal journey into all kinds of evil. You're living with bad human beings every day. All you see, hear, feel, smell, and touch is criminal and immoral behavior. Talking things out with a shrink keeps you in touch with the good of life."

The waitress walked by, and Mac made a circular motion for another round of drinks.

"Just a few more points, Janine, and then I promise, hand on my heart, I will hold my peace," Mac declared.

Janine couldn't suppress an admiring giggle. At that moment, she recognized why she loved her Uncle John so much. Despite all his "journeys into evil," the man had a profound sense of humanity and a unique goodness she had never realized.

"Please, Uncle John, go on."

Shooting Bogies

"You can expect support from friends and family," Mac said, "but their empathy and perspectives will be limited simply because they can't truly relate to what you do. Too many of us undercovers experience mental breakdowns. Some take their lives. That's why there's no shame in seeing a shrink. I check in with mine once a month. We're often perceived as tough guys by our colleagues because of the risks we take. But we're fragile human beings like everybody else."

Mac drained his beer bottle and declared, "That's it, Janine, the lecture is over. I tell you these things out of love, you know that?"

"I know where this is coming from, Uncle John," Janine said, "I love you too. Always have and always will."

Then Janine stood up, leaned over the booth table, cradled her Uncle John's head, and kissed him on his forehead. Mac just sat there and smiled.

"Janine," Artie said, suddenly interrupting Janine's reverie, "if you don't need me anymore, I'm cutting out."

"We're good here, Artie," Janine answered. "You can go. And thanks for your work on this case."

"No problem, Janine, see you soon."

Janine sat back after Artie left the conference room. She plunged back into her memory of her conversation with Uncle John. Had it been 12 years since they met at that bar? Since that talk, Janine had worked numerous operations undercover, all of them a descent into wickedness.

Uncle John retired from the NYPD five years ago and was living the condo Salt Life near the beaches of Venice, Florida. He was right on every point he voiced. The fear was constant. She trusted few people. She learned to acutely remember every detail of her alias.

Her personal life was suffering. She found speaking with her shrink once and sometimes twice a month comforting and helpful.

However, the most soul-searing element of undercover enforcement was learning to live with evil human beings 24/7. The evilness she witnessed over the years eroded her spirit. But the solace of working with good human beings like Artie Zimmerman, Paul Reynolds, John Whitney, and others in the office balanced the righteousness ledger. There were indeed good and honest people out there.

But the ethical equation changed as this Bogalinsky operation unfolded. Depending on your moral perspective, it transformed some of the good guys into bad guys, including herself. It wasn't something she could talk to her shrink about, ever. She would have to learn to live with and accept an evilness in which she would have a hand. An evil that her Uncle John hadn't touched on that night in the bar.

24

It had been eight days since Howard mentioned the Bogalinsky deal was set. That meant there were two days to go for the Fair Play closing. Rocky had been on pins and needles since his lunch with Howard, golf round with Rita, and meeting with Gino. Indeed, Rocky's anxiety was off the charts. He wasn't sleeping well. He wasn't eating—unusual for him. And forget about his golf game. It was in the toilet.

He was alone in a world that was upside down. Howard left town two days after his lunch at the Park View, Howard telling Rocky he had business overseas. But what Howard was doing, Rocky knew, was distancing himself from an impending murder. According to Pete Malone, Rita left New Jersey yesterday to fly to Florida to visit some old friends. And Pete himself was keeping his distance and seemed more aloof than usual.

Most unusual of all, Gino was as quiet as a church mouse. Rocky not hearing from Gino at all since their last meeting. But what more could Gino have him do anyway? The climax of Rocky telling Gino the deal was completed had been reached. Rocky's obligation to Gino was fulfilled. His penance for his social blunder at the funeral was realized. Gino had no more use for him. But strangely, Rocky was missing his contentious interactions with Gino. Rocky proved he could withstand Gino's temper and sometimes stand up to the little prick. Equally perplexing were his feelings for Bogalinsky. Bogalinsky returned to Fair Play several days after Rocky met with Gino. And Rocky, pained by old-fashioned

Catholic guilt, started having more kind-hearted feelings towards the guy.

Rocky was at his desk at the pro shop at Fair Play, turning over all these thoughts in his mixed-up head, when Pete Malone appeared at the door.

"Rocky," started Malone, "Bogalinsky wants to play the back nine with you today at 1 p.m. So be available."

"I'm around all day," Rocky responded. "Got nothing doing. What's going on? Any idea?" Rocky wondered why this sudden request from Bogie to play.

"Nothing special," Malone said. "I told him we retained a new groundskeeping vendor doing work on the sand traps on 15, and he wants to check on their work himself—typical Bogalinsky, having to micromanage his favorite hole."

"What's wrong with those sand traps," Rocky asked. "They seem fine to me."

"Several wasp nests are burrowed into the greenside traps," Malone said. "We want to get rid of them. Some of the members have been complaining."

Odd, thought Rocky. There were a few nests on 15. Those wasp nests were typical on New Jersey golf courses for this time of year. Even by Fair Play's exacting groundskeeping standards, calling in a vendor to eradicate a couple of wasp nests seemed like overkill. And no one, member or guest, had complained to him. But Rocky was content with not challenging Pete on this. Overseeing groundskeeping was Pete's deal.

After Pete left, Rocky thought about Fair Play's 15th hole. Like Bogalinsky, it was Rocky's favorite hole on the course because it was the most challenging. It was a short par 4 at 325 yards, but it was very tight, with many scrub pines, oak trees, and azalea shrubs lining both sides of a narrow fairway. Any slight deviation from hitting a dead straight shot off the tee or from the fairway was cause for a lost ball. And, to make the hole more challenging, two cloverleaf traps were abutting an elevated and crowned green, rimmed with a backside creek. Because of all these hazards, it was the number 1 handicap hole at Fair Play, which meant it was rated the hardest hole on the course.

Despite all these shot-making hazards, the green's setting was the most peaceful spot on the course, wonderfully isolated. Often, and when he was playing alone, Rocky would spend a few minutes soaking in the tranquility and quietness of the site, temporarily forgetting his recent problems before he moved on to the 16th hole. Like Bogalinsky, Rocky was interested in seeing this new vendor's work.

But today's play on the 15th hole would be far from peaceful.

It happened so fast. Rocky sat frozen in the golf cart, mouth agape. His heart racing in his chest. It was like the first few seconds of a car crash. The exact moment when you slam on the brakes while your car is whooshing down the highway, heading directly into the rear-end of the vehicle in front of you that, for some inexplicable reason, suddenly, inconceivably, stopped. It's brake lights screaming at you, imploring you to avoid a collision. As you screech toward the stopped car, time swiftly, angrily rushes by. Simultaneously, time and space stand peacefully, quietly, surreally still. All you can do is morph into a horrified witness to an impending explosion of metal and glass. You feel helpless. Frightened beyond your skin. Scared out of your head. Your life's images surge by like a frenzied, out-of-control movie projector rapidly flashing motion picture frames onto a screen. These feverish emotions were what Rocky felt as he witnessed the execution of Pincus Bogalinsky on the 15th hole of Fair Play.

Shooting Bogies

The day started with everyone full of good cheer and high spirits. Bogie was gushing about taking complete control of Fair Play as he rode with Rocky to the 10th hole. In between his and Rocky's golf shots, as they played each hole, Bogie asked Rocky his thoughts on how to make the course even better. Rocky could tell Bogie was on a high. As they rode up the 15th fairway, Bogie became even more effusive and enthusiastic about the possibilities of the potential of Fair Play. Staging a pro tournament here. Building an upscale condo development and world-class spa over there. Hiring a Michelin-rated chef to improve the quality of Fair Play's already top-notch kitchen. He had all sorts of plans. But suddenly, Bogie's mood darkened as they approached the 15th green.

"What the fuck are they doing!" Bogie angrily exclaimed as they rode up to the green. "They're tearing up the whole sand trap for a few wasp nests!"

Rocky looked up to see numerous Hershey-kiss-shaped mounds of sand covering the majestic green of the 15th hole. There was a small backhoe idling loudly near the right-side trap. A worker was sitting in the cab smoking a cigarette. And a deep rectangular trench was dug within the perimeter of the trap.

The work crew, all clad in black jumpsuits, had their backs turned to Bogie and Rocky. The gaping trench scarred the majestic setting of the green. The idling backhoe and the behavior of the boorish crew vulgarly disrupted its tranquility. Rocky was shocked at what he was witnessing. Not two seconds after his incredulous exclamation, Bogie jumped from the cart and ran to the crew, swinging a golf club.

Rocky froze as the crew suddenly turned around. He saw the face of Crazy Vinnie Bellomo staring him down. Then, the tallest member of the crew coolly approached the screaming, irate Bogie, reached into the fold

Shooting Bogies

of his jumpsuit, and pulled out a revolver with a silencer. He walked up to Bogie and calmly shot the big man square in the head. As Bogie fell dead, two other crew quickly dragged the body over to the trench in the sand trap and threw Bogie in. Seconds later, the backhoe operator began filling in the trench. Then, with the speed and dispassionate precision of a NASCAR pit stop team, the other crew members used shovels and leaf blowers to fill back the sand trap. It took them less than two minutes to bury Bogie. And there was not a granule of sand or blade of grass that was out of place. The 15th hole had been restored to its natural beauty.

Rocky sat in the golf cart, watching this commotion of grisly activity. He was dazed and frozen in fear. Then suddenly, he heard someone close by shouting at him. But he made no attempt to respond. Vinnie Bellomo's meaty hands, grabbing his face, jolted him from his stupor.

"Rocky," whispered Vinnie. "Get fucking moving now. You hear me, Rocky? Now!"

"Okay, Vinnie. I hear you. I'm hearing you," Rocky answered, his heart still thumping wildly in his chest.

"When the cops start asking their questions," Vinnie said, "you tell them the following three things: Bogalinsky got a call. He asked you to drive him to his private jet. You have no idea what the call was about or where he was flying to. Do you understand, Rocky?"

"Repeat it for me," Vinnie ordered. Rocky recited his cover story to Vinnie and repeated it several more times as he saw the tall hitman coolly wave goodbye to him.

As Rocky drove back to the clubhouse, still shaking like a windswept leaf, he heard the high-pitched whine of Bogie's jet racing down Fair Play's airstrip. And seconds later, he saw it lift off into the puffy, lazy clouds of a wondrous summer sky.

25

The news of Bogalinsky's jet disappearing into the Atlantic, just off the coast of New Jersey, was the lead story for print and local broadcast media in the New York and Philadelphia markets. The media harped on how the jet took off without a fight plan and its transponder turned off. Both infused a sense of mystery into the story. The bigger mystery to Rocky was how Gino pulled off such a deed. But he wasn't asking questions.

In addition to the story of a private jet lost at sea, the news media began reporting Bogalinsky was allegedly doing business with the Syrian regime. Just what that business meant was anybody's guess. Because Syria was known to support various terrorist groups, it was intimated by many news outlets that Bogalinsky was involved in arms dealing. While the story blossomed into national coverage, by the second week, other news stories broke, and the Bogalinsky story lost steam.

Through all this, Rocky was being interviewed by no less than a dozen investigators visiting Fair Play. These included investigators from The National Transportation Safety Board, the FAA, the FBI, the Bureau of Alcohol, Tobacco, Firearms and Explosives, several tire-kicking cops from the New Jersey State Police, and local investigators from Egg Harbor Township. Because Rocky was confirmed to be the last person to see Bogalinsky alive, he was deemed a "person of interest," though certainly not a suspect in Bogalinsky's disappearance.

Rocky was particularly anxious about facing the FBI and ATF investigators. However, they were more interested in Bogie's business deals than his being missing and presumed dead. Rocky survived each interview by sticking to the three-part alibi Crazy Vinnie Bellomo told him to say: *Bogalinsky got a call. He asked me to drive him to his private jet. I have no idea what the call was about or where he was flying to.*

Rocky repeated this bogus story so many times that he began imagining it to be true. In a weird, survival-mode way, he was more than happy to believe this illusion and displace the bone-chilling reality of witnessing Bogie's cold-blooded murder. The image of the hit was burned into Rocky's memory bank.

Compared to his face-to-face encounters with Gino and Gino's crazy mother over the last few months, being interviewed by government gumshoes was a cakewalk. The toughest bastard, though, was a guy named John Whitney from the ATF. He all but accused Rocky of having a hand in Bogie's disappearance. Whitney had an icy glare punctuated by steel-blue eyes and a Marine crew cut. But Rocky stuck to Vinnie's script and weathered the storm.

In fact, during a couple of meetings, several interviewers took great interest in the fact that he was the golf pro at Fair Play. Several even asked for practice tips, which Rocky happily dispensed. Still, the fact that he was complicit in Bogie's murder weighed heavily on his heart and mind—especially at night when his guilty demons took flight.

Meanwhile, Rocky thought about Rita every day. She must be devastated, he thought. Pete Malone said she was in Florida when she heard about Bogie's plane. Pete told Rocky she had decided to stay there and not return. Malone himself announced he was leaving Fair Play soon to move back to the Midwest.

Rocky had been waiting to hear from Howard for over a week. Gino called him once to cryptically ask how he was doing. The conversation was terse.

"You good?" Gino asked.

"Yeah, I'm good," Rocky answered.

"Don't mess up," Gino threatened.

And before Rocky could respond, Gino hung up. And with those five words, Rocky got Gino's message loud and clear.

As the weeks progressed, prominent news outlets began corroborating Bogalinsky's nefarious Syrian "business" deals, resurrecting what appeared to be a fading story. Crenshaw Securities came under scrutiny after it was discovered they were to be partners with Bogalinsky on the Fair Play deal. Fearing lousy press that would link them to an alleged arms dealer, Crenshaw withdrew its financing.

And so began the corporate stampede to disassociate from Bogalinsky and Fair Play. National Golf Equities, Fair Play's current management company retained by Bogalinsky and The State of New Jersey, announced they also wished to terminate their involvement. And remembering how they got stiffed when Fair Play's last owner defaulted, several major vendors either pulled out or initiated a cash-on-delivery policy.

To make matters worse, several prominent corporate members of Fair Play resigned their memberships, too. It soon became apparent that people were jumping ship, running from a foul-smelling odor wafting through a morning mist from Fair Play's lush landscape. Without Crenshaw and its investor group in the mix, the future of Fair Play was in doubt. With Bogalinsky's disappearance and probable death, ownership of Fair Play reverted to The State of New Jersey. It seemed everyone was running away from Fair Play, leaving The State of New Jersey holding the proverbial bag.

Everyone except Gino Lofaccio.

26

Janine Cortez was exhausted. The Bogalinsky undercover operation had gone on for over a year. It involved many twists and turns, including entering into an unseemly partnership with a New Jersey mafioso. When John Whitney first broached the idea of working with Gino Lofaccio and his crazy mother, Janine and her partner on the case, Paul Reynolds were outraged. The thought of the ATF Newark office working a case with the mob was deeply repellent. Their anger became even more profound after meeting Gino and Mrs. Lofaccio in the same conference room that Janine now sat in.

But John Whitney had argued some good points for a partnership. Gino's involvement provided cover for the Newark office on the remote chance word got out that the ATF was involved in liquidating Pincus Bogalinsky. If that were to happen, Newark would discreetly leak to the press that Gino had the motivation to kill Bogalinsky so that he could buy Fair Play. Artie, bless his soul, had Gino on tape saying precisely that. A potential double-cross on the feds' part was an easy slam dunk.

Working undercover as Rita Torrone, Janine had a front-row seat to Bogalinsky's character. There was no question in Janine's mind that Bogalinsky was a terrible human being—personally and professionally. As the Newark and Miami ATF offices uncovered after a year-long joint investigation, Bogalinsky was making a fortune moving arms to a Syrian terrorist organization. He did so through a byzantine network of shadowy arms dealers, gun shops, and shooting ranges in South Florida. Payments were then funneled to shell company accounts into the Caymans, the Bahamas, and Swiss banks. Worse still, there was solid evidence that Bogalinsky was supplying arms to a radical Muslim group in Jersey City. This discovery sealed Bogalinsky's fate as an enemy of the United States. That's when the CIA got involved. Soon, word came from the black ops higher-ups in D.C. that Bogalinsky should be eliminated.

At this juncture of the case, Whitney made the unusual decision of bringing in Lofaccio and his crew. After several trips to D.C. to argue his case, he finally got the green light. While working as a military intelligence officer in the Middle East, Africa, and South America, Whitney joined forces and formed partnerships with numerous rogue groups, from local warlords to private militias. What better non-government organization partner could the ATF reach out to here than a faction of the New Jersey mob? Especially with a guy who has a vested interest in making

Bogalinsky go away and taking over the Fair Play property. And as everyone agreed, the hit had to be creatively planned and perfectively executed. It was an ATF/CIA/New Jersey mob marriage made in heaven.

But the fed team didn't expect Gino to recruit Rocky Delmonico into the case to avenge Mrs. Lofaccio's ego and pride. And by pure happenstance, the emergence of Rocky's friend Howard Kinder getting involved in Bogalinky's financing was a twist Janine and the rest of the crew in Newark never saw coming either. These two guys were now loose ends that Washington wasn't happy with. Luckily, ATF Newark had them on tape discussing the impending Bogalinsky hit. So, Janine and John Whitney had leverage on both these guys to force their silence. All these thoughts were roiling around Janine's head when John Whitney entered the conference room.

"We have Kinder in interrogation room one," Whitney told Janine. "I'll be behind the glass while you and Paul do your thing. He asked if he needed a lawyer, so he's worried he's guilty of conspiracy to commit murder. Play that card, but don't go overboard, either. Take it to the edge, but we don't want to reveal that we have him on tape discussing a possible hit on Bogalinsky. We want to scare the shit out of him to the point he never utters his involvement to another soul for the rest of his time on earth."

"Understood," Janine answered. "I certainly don't want it to seem like we need him to keep his mouth shut because of our exposure here. But I will scare him by insinuating—without saying so—a conspiracy charge. He's a smart guy. He'll be able to read between the lines. Paul will observe and intercede, if necessary, as we go along. Let's get this over with."

Interrogation room one at the Newark ATF field office was like any other interview room: Basic drab furniture that included a long rectangular table and a couple of government-issued steel chairs. One wall featured a one-way window where John Whitney stood outside the room.

Howard Kinder sat alone, facing the window, wearing a navy blue golf shirt and tan khakis. His heart raced when he received a call that the Newark ATF office wanted to talk with him. As Kinder listened to the ATF agent, it sounded like the talk would be routine. Still, he remembered and became concerned about his conversation with Rocky at the Park View Diner. Given what they discussed—a possible, impending hit on Bogalinsky—he wondered whether to bring a lawyer. The agent, a guy named Whitney, said it wasn't necessary. So, while he wasn't buying 100% into the agent's nice-nice demeanor, Howard decided against it.

Shooting Bogies

Bringing a lawyer, Kinder reasoned, might signal some guilt or perhaps telegraph his knowledge of a potential hit on Bogalinsky. He was confident he could do this alone, having faced aggressive lawyers in corporate lawsuits. But he decided he would play dumb, shut down entirely, or ask for his lawyer if the questions got too sticky. Whitney told him that Special Agent Cortez would be interviewing him. For some reason, he imagined Special Agent Cortez as a short, squat Hispanic guy.

Janine's movie star beauty immediately struck Kinder as she entered the room. He was enchanted and intimidated by her looks, ironically the same way Rocky was captivated by Janine in her undercover role as Rita Torrone. Kinder sensed, however, that she was all business and a tough nut despite appearances—no nice-nice from her either. Howard braced himself for an aggressive round of questions.

"Good morning, Mr. Kinder," Janine began. "I am Special Agent Cortez, and joining me here is Special Agent Reynolds. We appreciate you coming in today. As special agent Whitney mentioned, we are investigating the disappearance of Pincus Bogalinsky. We have been tracking Mr. Bogalinsky for allegedly selling arms to foreign terrorists. I'm sure you're aware of the case?"

"I'm aware of the investigation," Kinder replied. "It's been all over the news."

"Yes, it has. Were you aware of rumors of Mr. Bogalinsky's arms deals when you funded him to purchase the Fair Play golf property?" asked Janine.

Paul Reynolds sat in one corner of the room. He smiled to himself as he observed Kinder slightly squirm. Janine was the division's top interrogator. She wasted no time making Kinder uncomfortable and putting him on the defensive.

"I was unaware of any rumors or any investigation into Bogalinsky during that time," Kinder lied. He indeed had read the Hunter report about Bogalinsky's alleged arms dealing.

Janine knew Kinder was lying to her but didn't directly challenge him. She wanted her questions to be more nuanced rather than outright accusatory.

"Didn't the firm you represented do their due diligence before extending their funding capital?" Janine asked.

"I was simply a consulting advisor on the deal," Kinder replied. "You would have to ask Crenshaw Securities what their due diligence protocols were while making this deal." Goddam Tommy Peters for pushing this deal, Howard thought. He should be here sweating this, not me.

"But as a former top executive at Crenshaw, you know very well that doing due diligence is part of the process of any deal. Isn't that right?" Janine asked.

"That's correct, yes," Kinder replied.

"So, at minimum," Janine continued, "one would think you and Crenshaw's financing group would have heard or uncovered some innuendo or speculation about Bogalinsky's illicit deals. It's well known that Crenshaw's corporate security and risk management units are top-notch. Are they not?"

"Yes, they are. But again, you would have to ask Crenshaw what their protocols were on this deal. As stated, I was an outside advisor." Thank God she wasn't asking about the Hunter report, thought Howard.

Don't push this point too far, Janine, Whitney thought as he stood behind the one-way window. Move on to Delmonico. The last thing we want is to get tangled up with Crenshaw's legal department.

"As Special Agent Whitney mentioned, you are not a suspect regarding Bogalinsky's disappearance. But you are friends with a Rocky Delmonico who, while not a suspect either, has drawn our interest simply because he was the last person to see Bogalinsky alive. You are friends with Mr. Delmonico, are you not?"

"We play golf together. Mr. Delmonico has been my golf instructor. We have lunch or an early dinner after we play a round. Our only connection is golf. We don't socialize outside of golf," Kinder replied, trying to create distance between Rocky and himself.

"Our investigation revealed you've traveled extensively over the past few months with Mr. Delmonico. What was the purpose of those travels?" Janine asked. "Did you meet with any of Mr. Bogalinsky's associates while traveling with Mr. Delmonico?"

Paul watched as Kinder relaxed just a bit as he listened to Janine's softball question. But Reynolds also knew that Janine always followed up with an aggressive follow-up.

"We played in golf tournaments when we traveled," Howard explained. "Nothing more than a weekend of golf. And no, I never met with any of Mr. Bogalinsky's associates, nor for that matter, any of Mr. Delmonico's associates."

"And would that include a person named Gino Lofaccio?" asked Janine, looking Howard right in the eyes. "You never met him or talked about his business with Delmonico?"

Paul Reynolds watched as Kinder tried to stay calm. He was half succeeding. But Reynolds noticed Kinder's jaw clenched and knew his gut was churning. Based on what they discovered on Kinder during their research, ATF knew this guy was the main defendant in an anti-trust lawsuit against Crenshaw several years ago. So Kinder had experience answering hostile questions during depositions. But squaring off against corporate attorneys was a world apart from facing an ATF interrogator obliquely accusing you of a murder conspiracy. Janine was doing what Whitney requested: Scaring the shit out of Kinder.

"I am not familiar with anyone by that name. Rocky never mentioned him," Howard replied, knowing full well he was stepping off the cliff as he continued lying to a federal agent.

"So you never heard Mr. Delmonico mention a Gino Lofaccio?" pressed Janine.

"No."

With that, Janine nodded to Paul Reynolds, who was now standing. Reynolds made a show of shuffling some papers, out of which he pulled an 8" x 10" black and white photo and handed it to Janine. She made a point of pausing while she studied it for a moment. Then she slowly slid it across the table toward Howard.

"Mr. Kinder," Janine began. "Is that you and Mr. Delmonico leaving the Park View Diner about two weeks ago?"

Howard looked at the photo, and his heart dropped. It was apparent the Feds were tracking Rocky, and he, Howard, had become part of their investigation. Could they have him and Rocky on audio tape if they had photos? Discussing an impending Bogalinsky hit Lofaccio was planning? All Howard was doing that day was telling Rocky about the deal. But somehow, the conversation evolved into something more sinister.

"Yes, Howard answered. "That's Rocky and me leaving the Park View after lunch."

"And what," Janine asked, "did you and Mr. Delmonico talk about at that lunch?"

Howard realized they had come to a point in their conversation that could be life-changing. He could be tried for conspiracy if he told the truth. And God knows what else they would tag on him. All possibly leading to prison time.

He had already lied twice. Now, he had to decide to lie again about his damming conversation with Rocky at the Park View. He quickly weighed his options: If he stopped talking now or requested a lawyer, he would be signaling possible guilt. On the other hand, he could win the day if he threw the dice and gambled that these feds had photos without audio. Howard reasoned he had gotten nearly to the top of Crenshaw by having balls and gambling on some big deals—so he decided right there to go all in.

"All we talked about was our golf games and the round we played that morning," Howard assured Janine.

"No talk about Mr. Bogalinsky?"

"No."

"Mr. Lofaccio was never mentioned?"

"No."

"Are you sure about that?" Janine pressed again.

"Very sure," Howard said.

"And if we questioned Mr. Delmonico about that lunch talk, he could corroborate what you said today?"

Oh shit, Howard thought. The idea of Rocky corroborating what he said today hadn't crossed his mind during the heat of the moment. He hadn't spoken to Rocky since that lunch because he was keeping his distance after Bogalinsky went missing on his jet. He felt confident that if Rocky kept his wits about him, he would tell the same story about that fateful lunch: all they talked about was golf.

Howard decided to roll the dice again.

"Yes," Howard said, "I'm certain Rocky can corroborate our conversation."

"Well, with that said, Mr. Kinder," Janinie said, "I believe we're all set. Unless Paul has something to ask?"

Agent Paul Reynolds, sitting in the corner, taking notes while sitting stone-faced, just shrugged at Janine's question.

Shooting Bogies

"I'm good, Agent Cortez," Paul Reynolds answered in his Wisconsin-tinged accent.

The same accent Reynolds spoke with while undercover playing Pete Malone, the "disgraced" general manager of the Fair Play golf club.

27

Five Months Later

That day in July, when Howard walked out of the ATF interrogation room, he was rattled by Janine's questions. While Howard desperately tried to hide his uneasiness, it was clear to Janine, Paul Reynolds, and John Whitney that Janine's head-game interrogation had shaken and unnerved him. They especially noticed a nervous bearing in Kinder's comportment after she produced the photo of him and Rocky leaving the Park View Diner. He went into knots when Janine reminded Howard that she and her colleagues would corroborate Howard's Park

Shooting Bogies

View conversation with Rocky. After Howard left the building, the agents agreed they accomplished their mission. They had scared Howard straight into a forever silence.

Less than a week earlier, John Whitney's similar head-game interrogation with Rocky went the same way, too. While agitated with Whitney's probing questions, Rocky got through the interview by repeatedly parroting the statement Vinnie Bellomo told him to say. Whitney smiled to himself as Rocky repeated his bullshit testimony. Rocky didn't know that it was Whitney himself who conceived this simple, three-sentence witness statement.

It was Whitney who meticulously devised and planned Bogalinsky's liquidation. His biggest challenge was working with a CIA tech team to convert Bogalinsky's private jet into an unmanned, autonomous plane that could take off, explode and crash into the Atlantic Ocean. The pilot, working in front of a flight console in an underground office in Virginia, received his takeoff order from one of the agents on the 15th hole of Fair Play. Once the plan was finalized and approved by the CIA Special Activities Division guys, Whitney spoke to Lofaccio. He told him he needed the mobster's most hardcore guy on the scene at the exact time of the hit for the sole purpose of having a familiar face to keep Rocky calm and focused. But most importantly, Lofaccio's guy was to give Rocky a simple statement once the inevitable interrogations began.

This was to be Gino's only involvement in the hit, Whitney told the mobster. Whitney and his team would take care of everything else. But Whitney impressed upon Gino that this "loose end" named Rocky Delmonico would be Gino's responsibility at the time of the hit and forever after that. Especially if Rocky failed in any way. Gino understood Whitney's implication. Thankfully, Rocky

Shooting Bogies

got through the slew of interrogations, kept his mouth shut, and everything worked as planned. The good news was that Howard and Rocky had been staying away from each other since Bogalinsky's "disappearance." Their friendship had evaporated.

Regarding the Bogalinsky disappearance, media coverage tailed off 30 days after the gun trafficking news spike. Now, five months later, the news story of Bogalinsky's nefarious affairs and his disappearance was as dead as he was. The NTSB initially determined that Bogalinsky's private jet had experienced a catastrophic failure 10 minutes after take-off. While bits and pieces of the doomed jet had washed ashore near Point Pleasant, New Jersey, Bogalinsky's body was never recovered. Further investigation had yielded no exact cause. And then one day, four months after the crash, which was premature for a crash investigation such as this one, all federal investigating activity ceased quietly.

Between Christmas and New Year's, a deal was finalized by Fair Play Homeowners, Inc. to purchase the Fair Play Golf Club from the State of New Jersey, which had re-seized the beleaguered golf course. Fair Play Homeowners' principal owner, as reported by the scant Christmas week coverage of the local New Jersey press, was a Belleville, New Jersey-based nightclub and waste management operator named Eugenio Lofaccio, who had alleged ties to the mob. But given it was the holidays, and everyone was caught up in egg-nog-laced revelry, no one raised a fuss. The timing of the sale couldn't have been better.

Lofaccio, one newspaper article detailed, planned on developing a 100-unit condo community on the property. When asked whether his plans included keeping the golf course, Lofaccio said plans were to keep the back nine holes as a recreational entitlement for the condo community.

Shooting Bogies

When asked why the back nine holes, Gino explained that his favorite hole was the 15th. "The majesty of that hole is just killer," Lofaccio said. Little did anyone know that Bogalinsky's body was interred 6 feet under a greenside sand trap.

At the end of the year, Special Agents Janine Cortez and Paul Reynolds were reassigned to new ATF Field Divisions. Janine was transferred to Tennessee and was assigned to infiltrate a white supremacist militia cell allegedly amassing a massive cache of guns and explosives. She was assigned to work undercover again, but not as Rita Torrone. Her new alias would be Karen Blass, and she would be working as a bartender in a suburban tavern outside of Nashville called The Lucky Six. It was a popular watering hole frequented by members of the militia cell. The agency hoped Janine would use her excellent undercover skills to work her way inside the group.

Reynolds was relocated to Miami to investigate further the gun trafficking activity that was the source of the Bogalinsky investigation. He, too, would be working undercover in partnership with another agent attached to the Miami field division.

John Whitney stayed on as Special Agent in Charge of the Newark, New Jersey Field Division. In mid-November, he flew to ATF headquarters on New York Avenue in Washington, D.C. Whitney received a special commendation in a private, closed-door ceremony for his exemplary work on the Bogalinsky case.

Special Agent Arthur Zimmerman, who had twenty years with ATF, decided to retire. Immediately after Bogalinsky disappeared, Zimmerman had put two and two together. As they worked the case, he became especially suspicious of Janine, John, and Paul's secretive posture. And he was astonished by their lack of interest in not investigating

Shooting Bogies

Gino Lofaccio. It didn't take him long to reach the only conclusion that made sense: the agency he was working for was involved in Bogalinsky's disappearance. And that they were in bed with the New Jersey mob. It was all still a hypothesis, but one Zimmerman could not countenance despite Bogalinsky's treasonous activity. So rather than force the issue with John Whitney or go to the press as a whistleblower, Zimmerman called it quits and kept quiet.

On his last day in the office, despite being a snowy December day, Zimmerman came to work wearing a tee shirt that read "Fish Die When They Open Their Mouths—But That's Not Me." Underneath the text sat a smiling, twinkly-eyed sunfish lounging underwater on a pool float with a cocktail. Nearby was a dangling hook. Artie hoped that Janine, John, and Paul got the message—though no one said a word as they bid him their goodbyes.

After his stressful interrogation with Special Agent Cortez, Howard isolated himself and retreated to his spacious mansion in Upper Montclair. Howard wanted to distance himself as far away as possible from Crenshaw Securities, Gino Lofaccio, Rocky Delmonico, Tommy Peters, Special Agents Cortez, Reynolds, and Whitney, and the whole mess that was Fair Play. He gave up golf and spent his time day trading and reading.

Although a good amount of time had passed, Howard was still stressed, waiting for a knock on the door behind which would be Cortez, Whitney, and a slew of law enforcement personnel. All coming to arrest him for conspiracy, obstruction, etc. But the knock or a follow-up phone call from the feds never came. He was still perversely interested in the progress, or lack thereof, of the Bogalinsky investigation. But he resisted the urge to search for news stories on his computer, iPad, or cell phone. He was loathe to leave a digital trail that the feds would discover and possibly use against him somehow. On those occasions when he would travel into Manhattan from his New Jersey home for a business or social lunch meeting, he would often stop by the New York Public Library on 42nd Street and use one of its computers to get an update on the case. What started as front-page coverage soon trickled down to spot news. Now, there was absolutely nothing being reported. He found this to be odd but was relieved.

And then, just after the New Year, Howard Kinder was approached by a headhunter offering him a CEO position with a Paris-based financial services firm. He knew his wife Judy had always dreamed of living in Paris, and she urged him to accept. While he enjoyed living in the New York metro area, moving an ocean away from a very sordid affair he inadvertently got himself involved in was a long-awaited and welcome deliverance. So, he accepted the offer after visiting the firm's headquarters in the La Défense business district of Paris. Now, he was counting the days to his move to France.

A move to Paris, or anywhere else, however, was off Rocky Delmonico's radar. He was left with hanging out in his house, alone. Howard deserted him and went AWOL. He never heard from Gino after that terse phone call in the summer. He saw The Pipe once or twice on the street. But outside of a quick hello, The Pipe just kept walking. Crazy Vinnie rode by in his car one day while Rocky was out sweeping the sidewalk in front of his house. When their eyes met, Vinnie gave him an intimidating "don't-you-even-think-about-it" nod. Rocky gulped and nodded back.

The person he missed most was Rita Torrone. She never reached out to him after Bogie's disappearance, and he wondered why.

Shooting Bogies

He reminisced often about the first day they met and the great round they played, topped off by being her party escort that evening. What a great day that was! He was troubled, though, by the memory of all the questions she had asked him when they played again. And he was still uneasy about his dream where she turned into a wicked witch. Was there something to this premonition, or was he just being superstitious? He chalked it up to the latter because he wanted to believe in her goodness.

Just after Labor Day, he resigned his Woodland Crest Country Club membership. Without Howard there as his friend and golf partner, Rocky found playing with other club members excruciating. Plus, he needed the big paydays of playing for serious money with Howard and his business cronies to afford the yearly dues and monthly fees. More frustrating to him was that he was losing rounds to hacks and duffers, players he had soundly beaten in the past. His game was in total collapse. He lost his focus on the tee box, fairways, and putting greens—virtually everywhere on the course. The image of Bogalinsky getting whacked not twenty feet away from him permeated his consciousness. The imagery became even more vivid when he stepped on a golf course. He felt he would be forever preoccupied by what he viewed as his complicity in the act. Indeed, his religious, spiritual, and superstitious senses compelled him to view his role and inaction as cowardly.

His profound guilt was especially manifested by the perpetual putting "yips" he was experiencing. Easy putts from a short distance away became horrible misses and caused embarrassment and self-ridicule. Missing putts was his penance, he convinced himself. Instead of racking up pars, birdies, and eagles and winning golf bets as he had

Shooting Bogies

done many times before, he resigned himself to scorecards full of bogies.

Bogies that would forever haunt his soul.

The End

Read on for an early look of Ralph Monti's next novel

MURDER IN AN HOA

1

Moses Moon

My name is Moses Moon. My parents named me Moses because they wanted me to be a "born" leader inspiring the masses, just like the Old Testament guy.

When I was growing up, I was encouraged by my parents to be president of the United States. But can you imagine a guy named Moses winning the electoral votes in states like Alabama, Kentucky, Mississippi, and Wyoming? Or even Indiana, Arizona, Texas, or Montana? That's 92 electoral votes lost before they start counting the ballots. No doubt, my parents had a very optimistic outlook on life. Instead, right after college, I opened a deli on Queens Boulevard in New York City that was very successful. I led, managed, and inspired cooks, servers, bussers, and dishwashers and listened to the sometimes cranky customers who complained about the pickle garnish or the fat content of the corned beef. As a deli operator, I was a success. But as a leader of the masses, I missed the boat.

After selling the deli and moving to Florida, I finally snagged my first and only president's title. I became president of my Homeowners Association. For those unfamiliar with living in an HOA, it's a community association that creates regulations to keep behavior polite, neighborhood aesthetics consistent, and property values high. Residents are elected to the HOA Board of Directors and then charged to govern the community. While HOA governance demands leadership, people, and business skills, often, a person is voted in because they are popular—skills be dammed. I was voted president not because I was popular but because no one else ran for office after a scandal that plagued the previous HOA board.

So, at 65, I became the Happy Haven Estates Homeowners Association president, which probably thrilled my parents in heaven. Unlike other presidential gigs, there are no perks with this presidency. No private jet, chauffeured car, luxury mansion, salary, or expense account come with the job. I'm lucky if I get an "atta boy" from my fellow resident constituents. It's a gig with minimal upside but lots of stomach distress, as my fellow board member Tiny Kolenski reminds me.

What's my job description? I'm tasked to lead, govern, mediate, scold, soothe, and cajole 133 Happy Haven Estates homeowners to (1) conform to the homeowners association's bylaws, rules, and regulations and (2) make sure all our homeowners keep their houses and property nice and tidy—in conformance to point number 1. After a few years on the job no one else wants, I've come to believe my Moses namesake had an easier time parting the sea and leading his followers to the promised land than I do satisfying 133 homeowners.

The good news is I get to share HOA leadership's chores and stomach distress with four other individuals who make up the Happy Haven Estates Board of Directors. It's an eclectic mix of personalities, but we all get along reasonably well. They are the aforementioned Tiny Kolenski, who, despite his name, is a monster of a man, standing well over 6 feet 4 inches tall and weighing in at 260 pounds. Part Ukrainian and part Polish, Tiny is barrel-chested with arms that look like hanging provolones you'd see at an Italian salumeria. Tony made his living as a construction superintendent in Chicago. He sprinkles every sentence with four-letter words while he chews on an ever-present cigar perpetually wedged on the right side of his mouth. Underneath his weather-beaten, gruff exterior is a honey bunny of a man. Or so his wife, Dolly, tells me. I've yet to see the honey or bunny of Tiny yet. Hopefully soon. Tiny serves as vice president of the HHE board.

Our Treasurer is Thomas Sygert. Thomas was born and raised in Wilmington, Delaware. He has a sallow complexion that befits someone who sat behind a desk his whole life. After earning his CPA, he spent 35 years as an in-house accountant at DuPont Chemical. He retired five years ago and raised his hand when the board asked for someone to volunteer as the Treasurer. No one in HHE knows much of anything about Thomas. He shows up at board meetings, gives the board and residents his monthly accounting update in a droning monotone, and then doesn't say another word for the rest of the meeting. He is the first to leave member meetings, and we never see him at community socials. He is a solid and honest bean counter but as personable as a Stop sign.

Midge Reynolds is the Board Secretary. Midge is a holdover from the previous scandal-plagued HOA board. Everyone else on that board resigned in disgrace or under a cloud of suspicion, except for Midge. She grew up on a farm in Iowa, slinging haystacks and cutting corn stalks, and has the muscles and a Midwestern work ethic to prove it. Her post-meeting Board minutes are always spot on. Her husband died several years ago. She lives alone in one of the bigger houses in the HOA with her two Greyhounds (Boris and Natasha) and a cat named Saline.

Finally, our Member-at-Large is Larry Walsh. Larry is a retired State Trooper from Columbus, Ohio. Larry is an Ohio

State University alum and an OSU football fanatic. He has OSU license plates, rear window decals, and a big OSU flag flapping in the wind in front of his house. Inside his house, his man cave is loaded with OSU tchotchkes, and his pool bottom is emblazoned with the OSU logo. You simply can't forget that Larry is an OSU alum. His other claim to OSU fame is he headed up the State Trooper security detail at all the OSU football home games for ten years. Everybody likes Larry because of his friendly demeanor. I also suspect some of our residents want to stay on the good side of Larry because of the 9mm Glock he sports on his left hip.

Helping the board govern HHE are several volunteer committees comprising other HHE residents. Our committee members do much work, more so than the board. They are a platoon of day-to-day field agents keeping watch on our community.

Ralph Monti

We have a Landscaping Committee that oversees the care of the common grounds and gardens and works with our landscaping and pond maintenance vendors. Landscaping is chaired by Dusty Phella, an apt name for someone who loves to play in the dirt either by himself, with other committee members, or when supervising our landscape vendors. Dusty is also passionate about the care and maintenance of our five lakes, which, in reality, are stormwater retention ponds. These ponds are critical to mitigate flooding in our community. Each pond feeds into a nearby watershed before draining into the Gulf of Mexico. Every community is required to be designed with a stormwater pond system. Real estate agents hate the term stormwater retention pond, so they sell them to unknowing prospective home buyers as lakes. Houses abutting these lakes/ponds always sell for a premium price.

I still chuckle when I read a real estate listing that terms a home as "waterfront," as if the house was on the Gulf and not facing a sophisticated stormwater drainage system.

A Social and Hospitality Committee plans monthly socials for our residents at our clubhouse, nearby restaurants, and the beach. Socials are an excellent way to meet new residents and develop an esprit de corps among year-round and seasonal residents. Alcohol is served so that esprit de corps can get too cozy sometimes. Like the evening when Jerry Marcus, the neighborhood flirt, tried to get too hand-chummy with a new resident's wife. Things got nasty quickly. Thankfully, Larry Walsh's friendly demeanor and police training to defuse a potential altercation calmed things down. The fact that Larry was sporting his Glock as part of his Tommy Bahama cabana ensemble helped, too. The giggly and gregarious Candy Shure runs Social and Hospitality. Candy was born to plan socials.

Despite her constant giggles that punctuate every sentence she utters and therefore grates on everyone's nerves, the woman plans great Friday Night Fish Fries, Tiki Night Pool Parties, and Sunday evening Drum Circles at the beach.

Joe Smith heads up our County Liaison Committee. Joe interfaces with the Sheriff's Office and any other County office that might have a statute that HHE must conform to. Joe is perfect for this job as he spent 35 years as a procurement analyst in Jefferson County, Indiana. With only a population of 32,000, I'm unsure how many procurements Joe had to analyze over his decades-long tenure in Jefferson County. But he indeed loves to wade into the waters of a bureaucratic snafu.

Dee Dee and Steve Wilkes are a husband-and-wife team who co-chairs our Communication Committee. Dee Dee writes and takes photos for our monthly e-newsletter, *The*

Happy Haven Estates Gazette. She can often be seen riding her dayglo-orange recumbent bicycle around the streets of HHE, taking pictures of the two-legged and four-legged wildlife in HHE. Some of these photos often appear in the Gazette. We all can recognize a Dee Dee photo. She has a propensity to have the tip of her pinkie finger intrude on the right side of the photo frame. The joke around HHE is if a photo doesn't have a pinkie tip, it isn't a Dee Dee. Her husband, Steve, oversees the HHE website and member database. He was an IT guy who worked for AT&T, and you can tell his passion is security patches, potential database breaches, web server errors, and passwords. No one knows what Steve is talking about when he updates his monthly HHE website at our meetings; we're just happy the website is up and running.

The two remaining committees, the Architectural Committee and the Fining

Committee are the most powerful in HHE and work closely with the Board. Jack Hurley chairs the Architectural Committee. Jack is a former Marine and a Vietnam veteran lieutenant who earned a reputation for running a tight ship. He continues that legacy at Happy Haven Estates.

Jack and his two other committee members monitor every resident in Happy Haven Estates to ensure they conform to the HOA bylaws. If a homeowner wishes to re-paint the exterior of his house, for instance, Jack visits the homeowner and advises the HOA-approved color palette. If a resident wishes to fly a flag in front of his house, Jack must approve it per the bylaws. He must review and approve any tree removal, shrub trimming, fence material (no plastic, only wood), or any outside house addition. HHE has bylaws that dictate the type of tree you can plant on your property, what kind of mailbox you must have, the color temperature and wattage of the light bulb in your lamp post, where you must place your TV receiver dish, what type of vehicles are prohibited in your driveway, when you're allowed to put up your Halloween and Christmas decorations, and a slew of other restrictions. They are all posted on the HHE website. If you're a nonconformist, an independent-minded spirit, or just a plain outside-of-the-box, creative thinker, then HOA living may not be for you. But close to 74 million people in America find comfort in living in the tedium of HOA conformity. HOA living is popular, especially here in Florida, where 50,000 registered HOAs are second only to California. I should mention that HHE homeowners can appeal Jack's ruling if they feel he hasn't interpreted a specific bylaw correctly. The homeowner can argue his case before the board, but Jack has gotten it right 100% of the time.

Katie McQueen was heading up the Fining Committee before her untimely murder. Katie volunteered a lot of time to HHE and fined a record number of residents. Like Jack, Katie was a valuable committee volunteer who kept everyone on their toes. She's a former Catholic school nun who was noticeably private and evasive about her past.

Katie's job as Chair of the Fining Committee was to troll the neighborhood to look for resident violations of the bylaws. If she spotted a violation, she would make notes, snap a photo (which never included a pinkie tip), and send a report to the Board. The Board would then send a letter to the offending homeowner telling him he had 30 days to remediate the violation. If the violation was not addressed by the deadline, fines and liens would be assessed.

On the first Tuesday of each month at 7 p.m. sharp, the board meets to discuss various topics, including financial updates, committee reports, resident appeals, vendor proposals, and anything else brought before the board. We meet at our community clubhouse. All homeowners are invited.

Depending on the topic agenda, which is usually emailed several days before the meeting, we typically get 30 to 60 homeowners to attend. One November meeting drew almost 100 homeowners, which was an all-time high. That night's agenda was a discussion to raise annual dues to $50.00 per homeowner. In June that year, the community suffered massive hurricane wind damage to its common ground trees and shrubs, ponds, and clubhouse fixtures. To pay for removing all the landscape debris, replanting, and repairs to the clubhouse and pool areas, the board was forced to tap into its cash reserves. To replenish these reserves, I proposed a slight annual dues increase.

Starting January 1 of the following year, the annual fees would increase to $850 per year, a bargain compared to other communities similar to Happy Haven. In a community with an average house sale price of $900,000, the board thought such a modest annual increase would pass without any fuss. Not so. One homeowner declared she would have to cut back on her grandchild's Christmas presents if such an increase occurred. Never mind that she drove to the meeting in a $90,000 Mercedes Benz. Another neighbor cried that he would have to fire his landscaper and be forced to mow his lawn under the hot Florida sun. Should anything happen to him while he mowed the property, this 87-year-old codger told his wife to sue the board for wrongful death. My board colleagues and I were criticized for fiscal mismanagement and harangued by so many homeowners that I proposed we immediately withdraw the increase. Smart guy that I am, I know how to read a room. Plus, I wanted to return home in one piece.

We never anticipated the uproar that ensued. The previous board's lack of financial transparency stirred up part of the uproar. In addition to incompetence, it was discovered that several members of the previous board were receiving cash and services rendered kickbacks from vendors hired to provide services to the community. The previous president was given a new in-ground pool by the same vendor who replaced the community pool. This was just one of many transgressions he and several of his cronies on the board received. This kind of graft is not unusual for HOA boards. The few laws they must follow are weak and unenforceable.

Missing in action that night was Jake Wong. Jake represents Omega Professional Property Management, a company that is supposed to be the board's partner in community governance. As the State of Florida mandates, every registered homeowners association must have a professional property management company to advise, counsel, and consult with the HOA board. We inherited Jake and Omega from the previous, scandal-plagued Happy Haven Estates board. Jake and Omega are in the third year of a three-year contract whose termination clause makes it very costly for us to fire them. Oh, I don't think I mentioned that Jake *is* Omega—it's a one-man show, even though his wife and three children are listed as employees on Omega's website. To say Jake is a disappointment is an understatement. He has essentially done nothing to earn his $1500.00 per month fee. Jake is a nice man, but he'd rather spend his mornings fishing in the Gulf, followed by ambitious liquid lunches at Jo-Jo's Tiki Bar in the afternoons, than answering questions from and working with HOA hacks like me. As far as his missing our tumultuous November meeting, rumor has it he was at Jo Jo's celebrating a huge fish catch that night. While we were under the siege of grumpy old crabs that evening, Jake was toasting the large school of groupers he reeled in that day. I can't blame him. I always preferred grouper over crabs, too.

2

Olivia Edmonds in Mexico (Before She Was Known as Katie McQueen).

Olivia Edmonds sat at a patio table waiting for Rogilio Della Cruz, one of Mexico's notorious drug cartel leaders, to arrive. He and his gang, Los Senores, or The Lords, were a brutal force in this picturesque village of Duasco. If you got on the wrong side of Della Cruz or one of his gang members, it was time to make the 60-mile trip to El Norte and start life anew. It was better to take a chance on being chased and caught by a group of gringoes, than to face retribution from a member of Los Senores.

Among their other demands, Della Cruz's gang members terrorized Duasco villagers and businesses by extorting protection money for them to leave you and your family alone. You were looking for trouble if you didn't pay your monthly share. But a surprising twist occurred last month when some villagers struck back. Wielding machetes and hunting rifles, the masked villagers confronted a group of gang members on a sports field in the center of town. They were desperately fed up with Los Senores' ultimatums. When the firefight ended, 12 gang members and three villagers were dead. After the Mexican media reported the battle, under blaring headlines that screamed, "Villagers Battle Local Cartel," the Mexican State Governor, Javier Gonzalez, announced he would station a base of 50 National Guard troops in Duasco to protect the villagers. "What they

Murder in an HOA

want most are peace and security," Gonzalez said at the press conference announcing the new station.

Olivia was understandably nervous while she waited. She was perplexed when a young man named Juan arrived unannounced at the door of her casita yesterday. He asked that she set aside some time today to meet with Senor Della Cruz at his house. At first, she was confused about who Senor Della Cruz was, but after she noticed his gang tattoo, she immediately knew which Senor Della Cruz young Juan was talking about. Why was Della Cruz wishing to meet with her, she wondered aloud to Juan. Juan said he would pick her up at 2:15 p.m. for a 2:30 p.m. meeting with the Senor. "Please be ready at the appointed time," Juan said, which Olivia interpreted, for no good reason, as a threat rather than a plea.

As she tossed and turned in her bed that evening, she brooded over what possible reason one of Mexico's biggest drug dealers would want to meet her. She was a volunteer teacher assigned to Duasco by the Houston-based Languages for Hope agency. Her mission was to teach English as a second language to the more needy children of the village. During her time in Duasco, she focused entirely on her students and carefully avoided discussing Mexican and US politics, immigration, or other hot topics.

Perhaps Della Cruz wanted to meet her to discuss last week's villager insurrection? Two of the masked villagers who were killed during the battle were the fathers of two of her students. Would Della Cruz accuse her of fomenting hostilities in some way? Of course, she would never bring Mexican troubles into the classroom and would gently deflect student questions about the tribulations of contemporary Mexico. She limited her teachings and discussions to English nouns, pronouns, verbs, adjectives, adverbs, conjunctions, and all the other elements that make up the English language.

As she contemplated all the possibilities of being dispatched to Della Cruz's hacienda, she took in a wondrous view. The house sat on the highest peak in Duasco. To the east was the town center, with its beautiful colonial-era architecture, including the famous Duasco cathedral and the Holy Spirit chapel, separated by a beautiful garden next door. On Tuesday afternoons, Olivia volunteered to work in the garden, tending to the Dahlias, Orchids, Morning Glory, Marigolds, Chocolate Cosmos, Mexican Passion Flower, and the Mexican Honeysuckle that blossomed there. She met many happy tourists who traveled to Duasco to visit the Cathedral and its beautiful Chapel and garden. But she also realized that Della Cruz chose this mountaintop property primarily because of its security against an enemy or a police invasion.

Taken in by the view, she got up from her chair and walked to the ornamental wrought iron railing. She was moved by the quaint beauty of the town and the beautiful mountain landscape beyond.

"It's a lovely view, isn't it?" a voice behind her asked, startling Olivia from her reverie.

She turned and was face to face with Rogilio Della Cruz. He was a notorious figure whose activities were constantly reported in the Mexican media. Like "The Teflon Don," John Gotti, who violently rose through the ranks of Mafia power in New York City, Della Cruz always escaped being convicted on charges that were brought against him. All of this added to his mystique. He stood before Olivia, wearing black slacks and a red pullover top. He was athletically lithe and handsome in a George Clooney sort of way. His salt and pepper hair framed a delicately featured face that, if embellished by cosmetics and a wig, could easily pass as a woman's. For this reason, the Mexican media mockingly nicknamed him "La Belleza" or "The Beauty." It was a nickname Della Cruz hated.

"When I was a young boy, I served as an altar boy at the Cathedral," Della Cruz said, motioning to the double-campanile building below. "After serving Noon mass on Sundays, my brother, sister, and I would play in the garden. My father died early, and my mother worked as a domestic for a family in Duasco. We were poor, so after our play time in the garden, we would walk to the cheapest cantina in town to split dishes of barbacoa and rice topped with mole poblano. That church gave me the fondest memory of my youth until things turned ugly with Father Castillo. Then, it cursed me with my worst memory. But enough of me. Tell me your fondest memory of growing up in Woodside, Queens. A place, believe or not, I visited many years ago."

Olivia was taken aback that Della Cruz would know where she grew up. But upon further reflection, she wasn't surprised, given that he allowed her access to his house and had the money and clout to check her background.

"My fondest memory," Olivia began, "is centered around my church, too. I vividly remember the excitement of dressing up in my white-laced dress for my First Communion. As a seven-year-old girl, I felt transformed, not only by the pageantry but also by the religious importance of the day. After receiving Communion, I felt closer to God. From that day on, I knew I would spend my life serving Him. I entered the convent after I graduated college. I became a teaching nun several years later."

"A nun who grew into a great leader," Della Cruz said. "You did ground-breaking work as the principal of St. Dismas School in Baltimore. I read about your accomplishments. Tell me, why did you leave the order?"

"It was time to serve in other ways," Olivia answered. "My work here in Duasco is very fulfilling. But why am I here, Senor? Surely, you didn't ask me here to discuss youthful memories and my past life as a nun."

"I'll get to that in a minute," Della Cruz said dismissively. "You know, I was always intrigued by St. Dismas. He's a saint who is not well acclaimed like St. Francis of Assisi or St. Thomas Aquinas. But St. Dismas should be recognized more widely as he represents what the Catholic Church truly stands for—repentance, and its counterpart, forgiveness."

Olivia was astounded by this man's comportment and intelligence. He was profiled in the media as a vicious cartel leader. That may be so, but she found Della Cruz an interesting and thoughtful man. It was wildly ironic that they were discussing St. Dismas. I wonder if he knew, Olivia thought, that many prison chapels in the United States were named after St. Dismas.

"Yes," she agreed. "St. Ditmas has been overlooked. As you know, he was known as "The Good Thief," who was crucified on the right side of Jesus. Unlike Gestas, the crucified criminal on Jesus' left who challenged the Messiah to save them all to prove He was the Son of God, Dismas asked Jesus to forgive him of his sins and to remember him in paradise. Seeing his repentance was genuine, the crucified Jesus granted him a place in Heaven. You are right, Senor, repentance and forgiveness go hand in hand."

"Well, Sister Olivia, it is hard for me to forgive," Della Cruz said. "And I blame the Catholic Church for that."

"And why is that, Senor?"

"Sometimes forgiveness is not part of the equation," Della Cruz responded. "I was betrayed in my youth by Father Castillo. I was a young teenager when my twin brother

Carlos killed himself. He left a note saying he was ashamed about what Castillo was making him do. When I confronted Castillo hours after finding Carlos, I put a knife to his throat to learn the truth. After he confessed and expressed remorse, I dug the knife deeper into his skin and ended his miserable life. I served five years in a juvenile detention center near Guadalajara. I never regretted not forgiving Castillo. But I admire those who can reach down into the depths of their souls who can."

"I'm sorry for what happened to Carlos," Olivia said. "These episodes of abuse are indeed a stain on the Church." Olivia did not reveal that this stain was a factor in her leaving the order.

"Let's have some coffee while I tell you why I asked you here," Della Cruz said, motioning Olivia back to her chair.

3

Moses Moon

As I mentioned, Katie McQueen headed up our Fining Committee. She was a by-the-book person, so the job of monitoring that every house in HHE was neat and tidy was a perfect fit. Most people shied away from being the Chair or being on the Fining Committee at all. Reporting on residents whose houses were not up to HOA bylaw standards is not a warm and fuzzy job. But Katie was a tough Irishwoman who worked in the toughest neighborhoods in New York and Baltimore. A newsweekly cited one school she taught in as the most dangerous in America. Teachers were mugged in hallways. Weapons were carried into classrooms. Nasty fights broke out daily in the cafeteria, library, and even in the nurse's office. The school represented the worst reflection of a ghetto: Daily violence, rampant drugs, and kids being adults way too soon. She had been through hell and back, as I was told by Jack Hurley, her close and only friend she had in Happy Haven Estates. Keeping things in order in a southwest Florida HOA community would be a cakewalk, or so Katie thought.

Several days after she was murdered, Katie was eulogized by Jack as a passionate and dedicated individual who was committed to anything she did. He said she never did anything half-baked and took pride in her work. She was discouraged and disappointed by people who wouldn't or couldn't measure up, especially those with advantages and the means. She saw the world as right vs. wrong. Rules were meant to be followed, or else chaos would ensue. There was never any equivocation or gray matter with Katie. These sensibilities were the heart of her volunteer work as the Fining Committee chair.

While previous Fining Committee Chairs kept a low profile when walking the neighborhood, Katie made no bones about her mission when she went out on her monthly inspections. She was equipped with an aerial surveyors' map of the community, binoculars to inspect roofs, a tape measure to ensure shrubs, lanais, and fencing were within house boundaries, and a camera with a zoom lens. She was always dressed in a bright yellow traffic vest and a bush hat as if on a safari. Which she was—a violation safari. To be sure, her monthly inspections caused a lot of tension with the neighbors. Many called her "Gestapo Katie," a nickname that got under her skin.

Katie cut an imposing figure as she walked the neighborhood. Her piercing blue eyes, underneath her cross-cropped gray hair, accented a no-nonsense face. At 69 years old, she was fit as a fiddle and quite buff for a woman her age. She would be up at dawn, rowing with her crew mates in the nearby bay. You could find her working out at the community clubhouse gymnasium several days a week. I peeked the one time I was in the gym and saw that she was lifting weights, much like a man half her age. In addition to her strength training, she would swim laps at the community pool and bicycle 40 miles on Saturdays. Despite her intimidating demeanor, some residents, angry because they were cited for a violation, would scream and yell at Katie as she walked by their house. Katie was chased and bitten by dogs that she claimed were unleashed intentionally, kicked in the shins by an unhappy kid, whom Katie knew was acting on orders from the kid's father, and chased away from a property by a low-flying, swooping drone being controlled by a pissed-off resident sitting in his backyard lanai.

If you saw Katie lingering outside your house, you would likely get a "Notice of Remediation" reminder letter co-signed by the HHE Board and our management company. This meant you had 30 days to address and remedy a violation. Common violations included dirty rooftops that needed pressure washing, broken fence slats, oil-soiled driveways, garbage and recycling bins stored in front of the home, un-mowed or dead lawns that needed landscape improvement, house exteriors that needed painting, broken light bulbs in lampposts, missing house numbers, broken mailbox posts, RVs or boats left in driveways, conspicuous TV dishes and antennas, tree limbs and shrubs needing pruning, and a whole other list of untidy violations. The idea was to keep the neighborhood in tip-top shape so home values stayed high.

While most residents acquiesced to the remediation letter, there were instances when a resident would push back and object to being told what to do. When that happened, we would have to contact our attorney and get more forceful by threatening a fine or lien. Now and then, the HOA board would end up in court adjudicating something as silly as fixing a fence. Almost all the time, we won our court cases. But not after unnecessarily paying lawyer and court fees. But that was life when you signed up to live in an HOA. There were rules you agreed to when you purchased a house in an HOA. Rules you were expected to follow.

As part of her Social and Hospitality program schedule, Candy Shure plans a "Welcome Back Snowbirds" Halloween party every October 31st every year. The timing couldn't be more perfect. Every October, massive flocks of snowbirds return to Florida to escape the chilly climate creeping into their northern nests. But more importantly, they return in October to add to the days they need to qualify for the zero-rate Florida State Income Tax. To be eligible for the lower Florida tax rate, they must spend six months and a day in Florida. One day less, and you lose your Florida residence eligibility.

You can tell the snowbirds are returning to town by the amount of traffic that begins to build up in October. Car carriers park along many main roads to unload fancy vehicles shipped from the north. After a summer of laid-back tranquility, it's a snowbird invasion: The streets have more cars, restaurants are packed, and the pace of life quickens. Some touchy Snowbirds bristle at being called Snowbirds. They prefer being called Seasonals.

This brings me to Moses Moon's Official Tribal Hierarchy of Florida Residency Chart. At the top end of the chart are the native-born and bred Floridians. They dislike just about anyone who moves or visits here, claiming we have ruined the beauty and vibe of their home state. Which, in many ways, we have. So, you can't say much, nor would you want to, when you see an F-150 pickup with a "Flo-Grown" bumper sticker or a window decal expressing something hostile aimed at the non-natives.

Just below the natives are the transplants, like me. Florida is now my and my wife's home state after being born and bred somewhere else. We've fallen in love with Florida's beauty and lifestyle—and are willing to withstand the oppressively hot Florida summers.

Next are the snowbirds or seasonals. In romance parlance, they are two-timers who reap the benefits of Florida while still having a can't-let-go affinity for their home state. Usually, grandkids are the reason they hang on to their northern nests.

At the bottom of the chart are the monthly and weekly tourists. The tourist invasion begins on January 1 and peaks by the end of March or early April. The higher tribes, at best, tolerate the tourists. A common joke among the higher tribes is to compare the native-to-Florida Gumbo Limbo tree, whose bark is red and peeling, to a skin-burnt tourist who spent too much time in the sun. They call it "The Tourist Tree." Most of us secretly wish the tourists would find someplace else to visit. But tourists spend tons of money (especially in ice cream shops and tiki bars), which keeps the Florida tax rate at zero. So, they are viewed as a necessary nuisance. And while there is tension among the tribes, we somehow get along.

But I've digressed.

Candy's Halloween party is one of the year's top events at HHE. That's because it's the opening party of the season. Everyone is in good spirits and eager for winter months of sunshine and fun. The party is at the clubhouse pool area. Everyone is expected to show up in costume, but there are rules. No risqué costumes are allowed. That means no revealing French maid costumes or sexy nurse get-ups on women. And no beefcake construction or police officer costumes on men. Since most of us are 55+ and counting, the reality of gravity and older age would suggest that risqué costumes are a non-issue. But many of us still have wild imaginations and distorted self-images, ergo the rules.

Cocktails started at 5:00 in the afternoon, and the party broke up by 10 pm, also known derisively as "Florida Midnight." A buffet dinner was served, and Candy hired a three-piece band for background music. I dressed as Sherlock Holmes and my wife Diane dressed as Dr. Watson. Everyone loved our costumes. It was a great way to kick off a new season.

But then, just after midnight, I received a call from a panicked Jack, whose voice was shaking. He told me he found Katie's body floating in the pool. I told him to call the police, and I would be right over. It's only a one-minute walk to the pool, so I arrived before the police came. Jack was disconsolate as we waited. When the police arrived, I realized I was still wearing my Sherlock Holmes costume. My wife and I were enjoying a postparty nightcap on our lanai when Jack called, and I hadn't yet changed. Despite Katie floating lifelessly in the community pool, I heard snickers and quiet laughs from several Sheriff deputies who found my Sherlock Holmes costume ironic and amusing.

It was an awful end to a festive evening.

Made in United States
North Haven, CT
05 September 2024